STRAW AND DIAMONDS

GETAWAY BAY RESORT ROMANCE, BOOK 4

ELANA JOHNSON

feel-good fiction

ELANA JOHNSON

ISBN-13: 978-1-63876-013-9

ONE

SASHA REDDING ARRIVED last to the beach, the group of women before her already laughing about something. Of course they had things to giggle over. Boyfriends. Dates that evening. Diamond rings.

She dropped her beach chair to the sand with a little too much force. Fine, maybe she threw it. No matter what, sand sprayed out and hit Esther on the right and Tawny on the left. Esther glanced up at her, her ultra-blonde hair practically white in the sunshine.

Tawny kept on talking as if she hadn't even noticed Sasha's arrival. And wasn't that the epitome of Sasha's life? She sighed as she sprayed sunscreen on her bare arms and shoulders and settled into her chair.

Tawny had recently broken up with her boyfriend. Or her fake fiancé. The fake fiancé that she'd fallen in love with. But even though they weren't speaking at the moment, Sasha knew they'd get back together. It was only a matter of time before the article in that poker magazine came out and Tyler—the fake fiancé/boyfriend—would come around and forgive her.

Sasha didn't have a fiancé, real or otherwise. Nor a boyfriend. Nor anyone interested in becoming her boyfriend or fiancé. It was a problem that, until very recently, all the women in the Beach Club had been dealing with.

But one by one, love had claimed them all. Okay, just three of them, but it felt like all of them to Sasha, as the other ladies were a bit older and adamant they didn't want another boyfriend or husband.

Sasha secretly did though, and when Tawny finally finished talking, Esther turned her and asked, "Everything okay?"

No, everything was not okay. Sasha didn't want to talk about it, but at the same time, she didn't have anyone else to tell. And wasn't that why she came to these little get-togethers? It wasn't to see the glinting diamonds, that was for sure.

"I'm taking a second job," she said. "Starts tomorrow." She stared out across the water, the winter sunlight still bright enough to hurt her eyes as it reflected off the bay.

"Things are that bad?" Esther leaned forward and peered at Sasha, obviously trying to get her to face her.

"Yes." Sasha didn't want to admit that she used money for her drink stand, The Straw, that she should've used to pay her electric bill. But if she didn't have The Straw, she wouldn't have any income. So she was a bit behind right now. She'd get caught up as soon as she started getting paid from this new job.

"What are you doing?" Tawny asked. "For the new job, I mean."

"I'm cleaning some rich guy's house," she said, the words like poison on her tongue. She'd definitely had enough of wealthy men, that was for sure. Stacey, Esther, and Tawny didn't seem to mind them, but Sasha preferred to meet a simple fisherman, or maybe a busboy. They, at least, wouldn't give her unsolicited advice about how she should run her business.

"Who?" Tawny asked, and Stacey and Esther looked more than interested too. Winnie, another Hawaiian woman in their group, kept her face placidly turned toward the sun as if she wasn't listening to the conversation.

"I don't know," Sasha said. "Jasper something."

"Jasper Rosequist?" Tawny practically screeched the name, which finally got Sasha to look at her.

"Yeah. Do you know him?"

"He's friends with Tyler."

"And Fisher," Stacey said.

"And Marshall." Esther's right eyebrow cocked, and a small smile joined the party.

"So what?" Sasha asked. "I'm not going to fall in love with him." They all knew about Newton and what he'd done to her stand, her life, her heart. No, she didn't need another man with money to come and shred everything she'd had to rebuild. Not again.

"So here's an idea," Esther said. "Why not just give him a try?"

"How about we don't?" Sasha glared at her friend.

Tawny nodded, more enthusiastically than the situation warranted. "You might like him."

"I don't care. Number one, he's my boss."

"And number two?" Stacey asked.

"I won't even see him. He made it very clear he works all night and sleeps during the day. I'm supposed to show up at six AM." She groaned just thinking about being up that early. "Work for a few hours—pretty quietly too—and slip out so I don't disturb him." She made air quotes around the last two words. "He's high maintenance already." The complete opposite of a busboy.

"So then we'll bet," Esther said simply.

Sasha growled, but the other girls didn't care. In fact, Winnie said, "I'll put in fifty bucks if she'll ask him out."

"I'll match that," Esther said.

"I'll double it," Stacey added.

"I'm poor," Tawny said. "But I'll put in twenty if he says yes."

Sasha started shaking her head about the time Stacey had spoken, but the thought of two hundred and twenty dollars had her reconsidering. That could pay for a lot of cups…or get her electricity back on.

"I'm not asking him out," she said, though the idea was still tickling the back of her mind.

"Well, if you do." Esther shrugged.

"There should be a time limit," Stacey said. "Within the first week or something."

"Two weeks," Tawny said. "Maybe she won't even see him in the first week. You know?"

"All right." Esther beamed as brightly as the sun. "Sasha has to ask out Jasper within two weeks, starting tomorrow, for a grand prize pot of two hundred and twenty dollars."

"If he says yes," Tawny amended. "I'm only paying if he says yes." She grinned at Sasha, who couldn't quite return the gesture. "Which I'm sure he will, because you're gorgeous."

"Fine." Esther looked from Tawny to Sasha. "Two-twenty if he says yes. Two hundred if she asks him, no matter what he says. We're all in agreement?"

Everyone agreed, except Sasha, who rolled her eyes and said, "I hate you guys," before facing the bay again and wondering if she really could make an easy two hundred dollars with a simple question.

———

The following morning, Sasha certainly didn't feel gorgeous. She wore her strawberry blonde hair in a high ponytail and tight-fitting athleisure wear that she could get sweaty in and not care.

Jasper had given her the code to the lock on the front door, and she tapped it in to the chorus of beeps. Something clicked and she pushed open the double-tall entrance. This place was ridiculous, and she waffled again on whether she'd even be able to look a man like Jasper Rosequist in the eye.

She was five minutes early, but he wasn't paying her by the hour. He'd said over the phone that he'd leave her a list on a table in the foyer each day, and she'd get paid five hundred dollars every Friday if she completed the jobs. Simple. Easy. Way more money than simple, easy house-cleaning required. But she wasn't complaining about the salary.

The table sat ten feet from her, a gorgeous display of flowers standing in a vase in the middle of it. She inhaled the fresh blooms before picking up the list for the day.

It read:

Welcome! Cleaning supplies are in the janitorial closet off the kitchen.

*Main floor bathrooms (2)

*Vacuum formal living, library, and great room

*All windows/glass doors on main level

Thanks!

So she definitely wouldn't be seeing Jasper today. He'd probably stay on the second level—or were there three in this house?—every morning when she came. She navigated her way into the kitchen, which held the scent of food without any evidence of anyone being there to cook it. No pan sat on the stove. No dish rested in the sink. It was like someone had sprayed the scent of buttered toast and scrambled eggs into the air and then disappeared.

She wasn't entirely sure what a janitorial closet was. She lived in a one-bedroom condo a block from the beach and only had two closets. One for jackets near the front door, and one in her bedroom. Though, while she opened one door and found mostly empty shelves, she supposed she had a linen closet too, if the floor-to-ceiling cabinet in the bathroom counted.

She closed the pantry door and tried the one next to it. That led to a mudroom, and another door that probably went into the garage.

The third door finally revealed what she was looking for: A bucket filled with cleaning supplies, brooms, mops, and vacuums in a variety of sizes, and several shelves with bottles of liquids and cans of powder.

Sasha decided to vacuum first, as it was a chore that she actually enjoyed. She could see the work being done, and she liked making perfectly straight lines in the carpet. As she pushed and pulled the vacuum over rugs in the library, and a light beige carpet in the formal living room, and a darker brown carpet in the great room, she yawned.

So she'd be tired. Didn't matter. This job would provide her with what she needed to keep her drink stand going and pay all her personal bills too.

She finished the windows and the bathrooms with only thirty minutes to spare, feeling sticky and sweaty despite the air conditioning filling the house. She wondered what on earth it would cost to heat or cool a place like this, once again glad she'd taken the job.

With her electricity out, she couldn't cool or heat her place, and she was at the mercy of Mother Nature. Not only that, but she hadn't had a hot shower in a week. With just enough time to spare before she had to leave to get to The Straw and get open for the day, she ran back out to her car and grabbed her bag.

She hadn't intended on showering at Jasper's place, but

down at the recreation center like she'd toyed about doing for a solid week. But he was sure to have hot water, and she wouldn't be competing with all the morning lap swimmers.

And he won't even know, she told herself as she tiptoed back inside and cast a long look up the magnificent staircase to the second floor. She hadn't heard a peep from anyone or anything inside the house. Not a squeaky floorboard, not a phone ringing. Nothing. So he'd never know she'd used his shower. She'd be in and out in twenty minutes tops, ready for a long day making tropical drinks and smiling at tourists.

Sasha made sure to lock the door behind her, and she stood in the hot spray as relaxation coursed through her whole body. Though it had only been a week, she'd forgotten how wonderful and soothing hot water could be. She just had to get the electricity back on—and soon.

She towel-dried her hair and cracked the door two inches so the steam would filter out. She hated getting dressed in the same room where she'd showered, as if Hawaii needed more humidity than it already had.

Even with the cooler air from the hall coming in, her clothes still stuck to her as she pulled them on. She'd just loaded her toothbrush with minty paste when someone said, "Hello?" and the door drifted open to reveal a tall, broad, sandy-haired man standing there.

Jasper Rosequist.

Sasha sucked in a breath. Well, it was really a breath full of toothpaste and water, which caused her to choke.

And cough. And spit white foam everywhere, as if she were a freaking rabid dog.

"I'm sorry," he said, moving into the already too-tight space and pounding on her back. "I startled you. You okay?"

Of course she wasn't okay. The heat from his palm against her back sent shockwaves through her system, and he smelled like he'd just gotten out of the shower too. One where he'd lathered up with pine trees and warm apple cider.

Her eyes met his for a brief moment, and Sasha thought sure lightning would strike her. She managed to spit in the sink—*so attractive*, she thought—and take a drink of water to clear the evidence of rabies.

"I'm fine," she said, her voice much higher than it normally was. "Sorry, I was…." She glanced at her bag, where certain unmentionables were still visible.

She practically dove onto the bag to conceal them, and when she looked at Jasper again, he'd backed to the doorway. He had to be perfect, of course, wearing a pair of pressed black slacks and a polo the color of the sky on a perfect summer day. If he put on a suit coat jacket, he'd be a twin to Newton, the last man who'd made her heart try to fling itself free of her body.

"You showered here?" he asked.

"I, uh…." Sasha didn't know what to say, and her pulse pounded now for an entirely different reason. This man had no idea what her life was like, and he'd *never* understand unless he had to live without hot water. Or air conditioning. Or the ability to keep food cold.

"Yes," she finally said, deciding to own it. Maybe she could still get paid for the cleaning she'd done that morning. "I showered here. I had a few minutes before my next job, and I was kind of gross from all the cleaning. It won't happen again." She gazed evenly at him, telling herself that he wasn't more important than her just because he had money and she didn't.

He said nothing for so long that Sasha's nerves started to fray. "Are you going to fire me?" she asked, lifting her chin and hoping with everything she had that he'd say no.

He just stood there, mute and growing more attractive by the moment as she took in the ripple of his muscles under his shirtsleeves and across his chest, the way his hair spiked in the front like he was trying to be the lead singer of a boy band, and the way he stood as if he knew he'd be able to charm her into doing whatever he wanted.

What was wrong with him? Sasha still needed to put on makeup and get over to The Straw, and with every second he stood there staring with those dark green eyes was another second she'd be late. So whether she found him attractive or not, she needed to break this guy out of whatever trance he'd fallen into. Stat.

TWO

JASPER ROSEQUIST HADN'T HAD a woman in his house in a long time. Okay, that wasn't true. His personal chef was female, but she wasn't interested in men. Somehow, Jasper knew Sasha was, even with the defiant glint riding in her dark honey-colored eyes.

"Hello?" She lifted her hand as if to wave at him, and he startled.

"I'm not going to fire you," he blurted. "The vacuuming looked nice. I thought you were gone." He wasn't a creeper. She'd left the bathroom door open. He hadn't touched the doorknob, simply pushed against the door with two fingers. He wanted to blurt all of that out to her, but sucked it back in. Wouldn't a creeper be sure to tell someone he *wasn't* a creeper?

Jasper didn't know for sure, and he didn't want to drive this beautiful woman away. His heart did a strange tango in his chest, and he couldn't figure out why. "You found the place okay? The supplies?"

Sasha, who'd showered in his guest bathroom, grinned at him, which only sent sparks spinning through his bloodstream. Oh, this wasn't good. His attraction to her was not good at all.

"Obviously," she said, pulling a makeup case from her bag, which rested on the toilet. "Did I wake you with the vacuuming? I did it first, thinking maybe you hadn't gone to bed yet." She whipped mascara onto her eyelashes, seemingly while watching him.

"I just got home, actually."

"Oh?" She turned toward him. "I thought you worked from home. In the middle of the night."

"I do." He didn't need to explain himself to her. What would he say anyway? *I had a really stressful night—lost over two million dollars in a bad diamond deal—and decided to go surfing at 3 AM. The pre-dawn waves relax me.*

Nope. He wasn't telling her that. Not only was it none of her business, it was simply too personal for him to share. He wouldn't even tell his father, who asked about the business he'd spent his life building before he'd turned it over to Jasper.

"I see," she said, though she obviously couldn't. "Well, I have to get to my next job." She packed everything up in her bag, and he licked his lips at the slip of black lace he'd seen on top. She hadn't wanted him to see that, and he'd put some distance between them pretty dang fast when he felt his blood heating.

"Same time tomorrow?" he asked, though he had no

idea what time she'd arrived today. The security cameras would tell him, but again, he wasn't a creeper, nor so anal that he had to know. He didn't need to watch her vacuum his floors or wash his windows.

He'd probably only keep her around for a couple of months anyway. His sister, Brighton, had come to visit from Paris, where she lived with her husband and two kids, and she'd said the whole place needed sprucing up.

"A deep clean," she'd said when he'd looked confused and asked what she meant. "You can tell no one really lives here."

Her words still rang in his mind, and it had been three weeks since she'd left. He lived there. He slept there. Worked there. Ate there. Heck, he even sometimes ran on the treadmill, right there in the house.

You can tell no one really lives here.

Her words had eaten at him, and he'd been contemplating his life for the past twenty days. He lived. Didn't he?

He wasn't so sure anymore.

Sasha paused in front of him, concern flowing through those eyes that ate him right up. "Are you okay?"

He fell back a step, his mind clearing without the orange-and-floral notes of her hair products in his nose. The air in the hallway was crisper too, cool and calm. "Yeah."

"I asked, same time tomorrow?"

"Yes," he said. "Yes, that's fine." He moved back further so she could come out of the bathroom with her bag.

Sasha gave him a nod and started toward the front door.

"And you can shower here any time you want," he called after her. He pressed his eyes closed in a long blink. Why had he shouted that? Did he have to be so obvious about everything?

She turned toward him and said, "Thanks," a pretty smile on her full lips. Something crossed her face and she gave her head a little shake. One eyebrow pulled down, and she said, "Would you...? Never mind." She resumed her walk toward the door.

Jasper practically lunged after her. "Would I what?"

She met his eye as he came up alongside her. "I'm really late. I'll ask you tomorrow."

He thought he saw a hint of redness enter her cheeks as she reached for the doorknob and scampered outside. He stood in the doorway and watched her fly down the steps and get in an older model sedan he hadn't seen when he'd returned from lying in Tyler's hammock.

In the next breath, she was gone, and Jasper retreated behind the thick, wooden door, his heart a jumbled mess.

"It's only because of the stress you're under," he told himself as he went into the kitchen to find the eggs and toast Jacqueline had made for him. He couldn't eat them, of course—what kind of savage ate cold toast that was five hours old?—and he sent another apology to her for not letting her know she didn't need to have his breakfast ready at five-thirty the way she usually did.

It's fine, she answered for the second time.

Take tomorrow off, he told her, and she accepted. He could pour a bowl of cereal as well as the next man.

He wandered upstairs and stripped off the clothes he'd put on after his own shower. After all, he didn't think he should go downstairs and check on the strange noises he'd heard in the nude.

"That would've been a disaster," he mumbled to himself as he fell into bed wearing only his boxers. With the bad business overnight and the way his heart was lecturing him about Sasha, it was a miracle he was able to fall asleep at all.

———

Jasper loathed cooking for himself. Probably because he couldn't find a frying pan to save his life. In his own kitchen. There was precious little food in the pantry and fridge, but he managed to find a package of hot dogs. No buns though.

And while he was an hour from climbing back into bed after working all night, his favorite sushi place wasn't open. His backward schedule had some definite draw-backs, including limited take-out choices and the inability to meet normal women.

Although…his mind wandered to Sasha, and the antici-pation of seeing her again kept his exhaustion at bay. He hadn't slept great yesterday after she'd left, those eyes following him into his dreams.

Which was ridiculous really. He knew nothing about

her. "Yet you hired her sight unseen to clean your house. Gave her access to the whole thing."

Maybe he was too trusting. Lara had certainly taken advantage of him. He pushed her from his thoughts at the same time he gave up on trying to find something to eat in his own house. He opened the drawer beside the fridge—which housed all his favorite energy drinks, bottled water, and more soda than a human should ever consume—and pulled out a stack of take-out menus.

After leafing through them, he tossed them back in the drawer. "Why do I even have these?" None of them were for places that were open. He toyed with the idea of texting Sasha. She did work for him....

He put the idea out of his mind. Jasper didn't need to come off as a self-absorbed, stuck-up guy who didn't get out of his mansion much, even if it was true. Maybe just the not-getting-out-of-his-house part. He *could* benefit from leaving the premises more often.

Opening the fridge again, he muttered, "You go to the Nine-0 meetings." He glanced at the door and saw a carton of eggs. He could probably put together a plate of eggs and toast himself.

He cracked and whisked and found a frying pan in the fifth cupboard he opened. "And the beach," he continued talking to himself. "And out to dinner everyday. Okay, sometimes."

His breakfast came at dinnertime, and his routine of waking, showering, checking email and his schedule for the day was almost as easy as breathing. He left the house then, usually, and went to grab something to eat. Sometimes he ordered in, as evidenced by the take-out menus that were for places closed in the morning.

Something didn't smell right, and he spun back to the stove. Smoke lifted from the pan, and he hadn't even poured the eggs in yet. He frowned, trying to figure out what to do. Oil? Butter?

He yanked open the fridge and couldn't see anything of the sort. So he grabbed the bowl where he'd cracked a few eggs and dumped them into the hot pan.

A searing, scorching sound lifted into the air, and the eggs started to boil. *Boil.* That certainly wasn't right, and the smell went from a little bit of metal smokiness to downright disgusting burnt egg stench.

He actually gagged and pulled the pan off the flame, hoping that would help. It didn't, but the eggs settled into an even surface. No way he could eat them though. He'd never eat in this house again, actually, not with that horrible aroma hanging around.

Laughter sounded behind him and he turned toward the arched entryway to find Sasha standing there in a dark gray pair of leggings that emphasized the length of her legs, and an equally form-fitting top in the same color, with a slash of bright blue across the stomach and chest.

He pulled in a breath, regretting it when that over-cooked egg smell got trapped in his nostrils.

"It's nice to know you can't cook," she said, putting her bag on the kitchen counter with a smile that showed her perfectly white teeth.

"We all have flaws," he said, moving to block the

offending eggs. He wondered how he could find out hers without coming on too strong or being a jerk.

She lifted the list and asked, "You have a theater room in the basement?"

He nodded with a shrug attached. "I'm having a party on the weekend." *You should come.* Could he say that? To his housekeeper of two days? Didn't feel like it, and he bit the invitation back.

Her face tightened, and the smile disappeared. "I'm still okay to shower after I finish?"

"Of course. I'll put a new towel in there." Panic poured through him. He might have to text Jacqueline and find out where the clean towels were. They somehow showed up in Jasper's bathroom each week, and while he did know where the washer and dryer were, Jacqueline took care of laundry and food. And cooking.

She couldn't stay in the mornings to do the cleaning she'd been doing for a decade because her son had just been diagnosed with diabetes, and she needed to be home with him in the mornings to check his sugar levels, administer insulin, and take him to doctor's appointments.

So she came early-early in the morning and made his breakfast, and she'd been coming on Sunday afternoons—he thought. He was pretty sure it was Sunday that his laundry was taken and then brought back folded and smelling like the tropical flowers Hawaii boasted to the world.

"I'm gonna head up to bed," he said.

"I'll be quiet."

"Oh, you'll be in the basement. I won't hear you if you close the door."

"Oh yeah? Pretty good soundproofing down there?"

"The best," he said before he realized it probably sounded like bragging. "I mean—didn't you want to ask me something yesterday?" The thought of what she could possibly want from him had plagued him since he'd woken late yesterday afternoon.

He bit back a yawn as she studied him.

"Yeah, um, about that." She shifted her feet and tucked a non-existent piece of hair behind her ear. "I was just thinking it would be nice if we got to know each other a little bit more. I mean, I'm working here now, and I don't even know you."

He blinked and stared, everything he'd speculated about flying out of his head. He hadn't expected her to *ask him out*.

"Like, maybe just coffee or something," she hastened to add. "So these little exchanges aren't so awkward." She gave a nervous giggle and clenched her arms across her middle.

"Yeah, sure, I drink coffee." He gave himself a mental shake. I drink coffee? He drew in a deep breath and tried to figure out how to interact with a woman again. It had been a long time for him, and his last relationship had been with a fellow Nine-0 member and utterly boring. Before that, he'd found all of his girlfriends online as he spent an astronomical amount of time on the computer and Internet for work.

And chatting through an app or even text was not the

same as being face-to-face with a woman with his heart crashing against his ribs like waves against the lava cliffs on the other side of the island.

She smiled, the gesture lighting the whole kitchen, and ducked her head. "All right. Coffee. You've got my number." She moved past him effortlessly and collected the bucket of supplies and the vacuum.

He simply watched, maybe a little stalkerishly. Jasper jumped into motion as she lugged everything toward him. "Let me help you." He took the vacuum and led her to the doorway behind the main staircase that led into the basement. "Here we go."

A blast of stale air hit him when he opened the door, and he honestly wasn't sure which was worse—that or the burnt egg smell still filling the house.

With the vacuum at the bottom of the steps and Sasha getting to work, Jasper climbed back to the main floor and then up to his private suite on the second floor, one more item on his to-do list before he could sleep: Invite people over for the party this weekend.

THREE

SASHA FINISHED WIPING the order counter, where sticky rings from her fruity drinks always seemed to be. It was mid-afternoon, and a lull had hit. Tawny had texted that morning after her beach yoga class.

A simple message, really. *So? Beach Club at three. Update wanted.*

And Sasha had an update. She tossed the washcloth into the sink at the back of the stand and untied her apron. "Maddy, I'm running out for an hour. You'll be okay?"

The thirty-year-old Polynesian woman waved the hand holding the knife. She tossed a smile over her shoulder and said, "Go. I'll be fine," and continued chopping pineapple.

Relief rushed through Sasha that she'd found Maddy last summer. The woman had saved Sasha so much stress when it came to The Straw. She worked hard, and she never called in sick, was never late, and Sasha never worried about her taking money from the till while she was gone.

She jumped in her car and drove around the curve in the island to another inlet, this one busier than the one where The Straw sat. A line stretched in front of Two Coconuts, another drink stand and her biggest competition.

But not really. Since they were on different beaches, it wasn't like she lost customers to them. But when Fisher DuPont had built his huge hotel on this bay instead of the adjoining one, he automatically brought more vacationers, tourists, and thus customers, to Two Coconuts.

She eyed the other drink stand, suddenly thirsty, and cast a look toward the bay to see if her friends had shown up yet. It didn't look like it, so she joined the line and studied the menu. "Guava and banana?" She shook her head. Didn't Mo know that combination would make people sick?

Not your job, she chanted as she inched forward. "I'll take the Fruity Foursome," she said. "Large. Frozen, with a straw."

The girl smiled at her and rang up her purchase while calling the order over her shoulder. Sasha tried not to look like she was drinking in the details of the inner workings of the shop. But Mo wasn't there, and this teen girl had probably just come on after her last high school class for the day.

Sasha paid and stepped to the side, still watching the people inside the hut. It wasn't bigger than The Straw, but

Mo had four people working at the moment, and they had better blenders than she did. Her Fruity Foursome took about five minutes before it was handed to her in a tall, slim Styrofoam cup to keep it cold.

She took a sip of the tart and sweet combination, glad she hadn't opted for something new. She loved this combination of orange, strawberry, banana, and mango, and she'd put something similar on her menu over a year ago.

The sun didn't feel particularly warm that day, and a bit of cloud cover had moved in. Sasha gazed out over the bay, her absolute favorite place in the whole world. The warm sand covered her sandaled feet as she headed toward the Beach Club's usual spot on the edge of Sweet Breeze's private beach, and she found Esther there already.

"Hey." Sasha dropped to the sand beside her. "Am I early?"

"No, they're running late," she said. "I guess Stacey had some problem in the gardens and Tawny's locking up her bike." Esther reached over and stroked back Sasha's loose hair. "You okay?"

Sasha appreciated the gesture. Though Esther was only a few years older than her, she felt like a wiser older sister. Sasha had never kept anything from her, but she hadn't told anyone about her financial troubles. Not even the women in the Beach Club.

A few minutes later, Tawny gave an exaggerated sigh as she laid out her towel. "There must be some sort of convention at Sweet Breeze. There's so many people on the trails."

"There is," Esther said. "Something about eye doctors. Researchers? Something." She focused on her phone and Sasha watched Stacey as she came down the beach.

As soon as she arrived, Sasha would be expected to give the update. Winnie had texted to say she couldn't make it but wanted to know if she needed to drop off her fifty dollars.

Stacey had barely arrived when Tawny pulled a twenty dollar bill from her beach bag and waved it around. "So?"

Sasha grinned and made a grab for the money. Tawny yanked it away, her eyes bright and teasing.

"That's mine," Sasha said.

"Really?" Tawny laughed and handed it over. "He said yes?"

"How did you ask him?" Stacey asked.

"I suggested coffee," Sasha said. "And made it sort of like 'hey, I don't know you at all, but you're asleep upstairs while I work, and it's kind of awkward.'" Sasha lifted one shoulder in a shrug and took another drink of her smoothie. "He said he drank coffee. I'm waiting for him to text me for when we'll go."

"He hasn't texted you yet?" Esther asked.

"He sleeps during the day," Sasha said, a pinch starting just behind her lungs. That was why she hadn't heard from him yet. "But he said yes." She waggled her fingers. "So pass over the cash."

Stacey and Esther both handed her their money with wide smiles on their faces. "That's great," Stacey said. "Really, Sasha. What if you guys end up falling in love?"

Sasha scoffed, the idea absolutely ridiculous. So maybe Jasper was *ridiculously* good-looking. And she found it hilarious and endearing that he couldn't even scramble eggs, though she supposed her natural talent in the kitchen didn't extend to everyone.

"It's just coffee," she told her friends—and herself—as she folded the cash and put it in her pocket. If she left now, she could get over to the electric company and pay her bill before she had to be back at The Straw.

She started to stand and her phone chimed.

"Is that him?" Tawny asked, her voice carrying too much interest.

"I'm sure it's—" Sasha cut off as she saw Jasper's name on the screen. "He said, how about coffee tonight?"

"Tonight?" Tawny jumped up and took Sasha's phone from her. She read the message as if she didn't believe Sasha and then asked, "Are you free tonight?"

"I'd need to talk to Macey, and it depends on how busy we are."

"You can sneak away for an hour." Tawny started tapping on the screen, dictating as she went. "I have to check with my staff." She wiggled her eyebrows under her sunglasses. "See? You're the boss, but you're a nice person too."

"Thanks, Tawny," Sasha said in a monotone. But honestly, she was glad someone else was responding, because she honestly couldn't believe he'd said yes. That he'd texted. That she'd even asked him in the first place.

"And it might be later. Like eight or so." Tawny

glanced up, a question riding her brows now. "Is that a good time?"

"We're pretty dead by eight in the winter," Sasha confirmed. "We sometimes get a rush about nine, once people finish dinner, but eight should be okay."

Tawny nodded and bit her lip as she kept typing. She finished and said, "I have to talk to my staff. And it might be later, like eight or so. And I can probably only sneak away for an hour or so. Doable?"

"He works at night," Sasha said. "I wonder what time that will be wherever he works."

"He'll make it work," Tawny said.

"How do you know?"

She turned her phone toward Sasha. "That's what he said." She beamed as she swept the phone in front of Esther and Stacey. "Oh." She brought the phone back to her eyes as it finished chiming.

"He's looking forward to it."

Sasha took her phone back to make sure the messages weren't pranks. Genuine surprise ran through her and she allowed herself to smile. "You know what?" She glanced around at her friends. "I'm looking forward to it too."

"Okay, so here's the next bet," Esther said.

"Next bet?" Sasha froze halfway through turning to leave. "I have to get going."

"Oh, you've got five more minutes." Esther grinned at her, those mirrored sunglasses doing nothing to disguise the mischievous quality of her gaze.

"I already asked him out."

"Yes, and now you've entered the next stage." She looked at Stacey, who grinned wolfishly too.

"I'm not taking another bet." The money she'd already collected from her friends felt like a brick in her pocket. "I have to go." She stared to walk away.

"I'll text you the bet!" Esther called after her. Sasha lifted her hand to indicate she'd heard, but she didn't stop or turn back.

Ten minutes later, she stood at the payment counter at the electric company, all the money she'd just gotten from her friends in front of her. "What do you mean it's not enough?" She was tired of going home in the dark, using the flashlight on her phone as a warped version of candlelight.

"I'm sorry, ma'am. You owe more than one hundred and seventy dollars."

"How much do I need to get my service turned back on?"

She tapped, a semi-genuine look of sympathy on her face. "Three hundred and four dollars and sixty-one cents. That includes the twenty-five dollar reconnect fee, and all the current charges on the account."

Three hundred dollars. It might as well have been three thousand. Sasha eradicated the thought, because it wasn't true. By Friday, she'd have all of that and more. "Okay, thank you." She picked up the bills and stuffed them back in her pocket.

"Would you like me to print you this so you have it?"

"Sure." While the woman did that, Sasha's phone chimed. A text from Esther that said: *New bet. $100 if you* *get Jasper to tell you the name of one of his ex-girlfriends during your coffee date tonight.*

With Winnie's fifty dollars and that one hundred, Sasha could have her electricity back by tomorrow morning. She pressed her teeth together and took the printout from the woman showing how much she owed, determined to win another bet in just a few short hours.

FOUR

JASPER LEFT his car with the valet and buttoned his suit coat as he stepped through the double-wide automatic doors of Fisher's hotel. While Jasper had lived on the island and enjoyed Getaway Bay for the past decade, things had definitely gotten more interesting since Fisher DuPont had showed up.

He'd brought the billionaires in the bay area together, and Jasper hadn't realized how isolated he'd become in the big house on the hill. Well, maybe he had. But he hadn't known what to do about it.

Now he had friends, and a reason to leave the house during daylight hours, and business partners that had strengthened his own company. Contacts outside of his own. He'd tried dating Lexie Keller, a fellow member of the Hawaii Nine-0 Club, but there was simply no spark there. He caught her eye from across the lobby, and she lifted her champagne flute in hello and quickly turned her attention back to the man she stood beside.

The lobby swarmed with activity, as per Sweet Breeze's usual—in the summer. But in January, this was most unusual. A large sign advertising where the optometrist dinner was being held caught his eye, and it all made sense. Fisher had wanted to expand his facilities to include a conference center, and he'd obviously booked his first group.

Jasper maneuvered through the people and waited for an elevator. His friends were meeting in a private room in the aquarium, where dinner would be laid out. Jasper hoped Lawrence would be there already, and he'd have a few minutes to talk to the man about how to move money without drawing government attention.

Not that Jasper needed to do anything nefarious. He just needed to be able to put money in the smartest places possible, and hopefully avoid the wrath of his father once the man found out about the blunder Jasper had committed on Monday.

He and Lexie stepped off the elevator together on the fourth floor and the attendant standing at the entrance of the aquarium lifted a blue velvet rope on the right side of the doorway and gestured them down a hall.

"Enjoying the new year?" he asked her, ever the gentleman and having nothing of importance to say to her.

"It's been great," she said, flashing him a tight smile. "You?"

"Great," he echoed, stepping in front of her to open the door. The scent of browned beef and salt and something sweet met his nose as she walked past him. He entered after her, relieved when he saw Lawrence talking to Ira, both of them with drinks already in their hands.

Another woman hovered nearby, clutching a glass she wasn't sipping from. She was new, and Fisher had been sniffing out the new additions to Getaway Bay that had enough zeroes in their bank accounts.

He caught up to Lexie just as she paused in front of the new arrival. "Gabi?"

Gabi's relief was like a scent on the air, mingling with the smell of roasted baby carrots and saffron rice. "Lexie. So good to see you again." The two women embraced quickly, and Lexie indicated him.

"This is Jasper Rosequist. He deals in diamonds. Gabriella Rossi, cruise ship heiress."

"Gabriella." He shook her hand, again, not a spark anywhere in sight though she was beautiful and elegant and rich.

So there really was something special between him and Sasha. Something he probably shouldn't ignore, or deal with for a single hour over coffee. His brain worked through possible ways to get her to go out with him while small talk was made between the women.

When it seemed polite enough to do so, he eased away from them and joined Lawrence and Ira. "Hey," he said, meeting both of their gazes.

"Jasper." Lawrence grinned at him hugely, the man more of a shark than Jasper liked to admit. "How are you?"

"I need some advice, actually." He glanced at Ira, who

owned real estate in thirty-one of the fifty states. There was some real money in real estate. And finance, as evidenced by Lawrence's wealth.

"Oh, advice." Lawrence kept the smile on his face as he threw back the rest of his soda. "Shoot."

Giving advice was Lawrence's favorite thing to do, and maybe for the first time, Jasper was glad for it.

"So let's say you've got a large sum of money in an account in Belgium, and you'd like that money to move through Switzerland to be taxed. Can that happen?"

"Depends on when the money is paid," Lawrence said. "From your company to another based in Switzerland? Sure, it's subject to Swiss taxes."

Jasper nodded. "And if it's just moving from bank to bank in Belgium before that happens?"

"You don't pay taxes until the money is paid," Lawrence said.

"That's what I thought." Jasper frowned. "But I got a notice on Monday from the Belgium Tax Commission, and they insist I owe them millions on unreported income."

Lawrence sobered and tossed his can in a recycling bin nearby. "That's not right. Do you have documents? I can come look at them with you. See what's going on."

Another dose of relief spread through Jasper. That was the offer he'd been hoping for. "Thanks, Lawrence. That would be awesome."

"Tonight? After this?" He swept his hand toward the buffet as the door opened and Fisher and Marshall walked through it.

"Oh, I can't tonight," Jasper said. As it was, he'd have

to eat and hope Fisher wasn't feeling particularly loquacious tonight. "I have a date."

He might as well put his mouth on a microphone and screamed the last sentence. It felt like every eye in the place—and there weren't that many—landed on him.

"A date?" Lawrence laughed and clapped Jasper on the shoulder. "I didn't know you left that hideaway of yours for more than dinner and these meetings."

Jasper laughed off the assessment, even if he was right. His sister's words flowed through his mind again, and he said, "Well, I'm trying to mix things up a little."

Marshall planted himself directly beside Jasper and leaned in. "You're going out with Sasha Redding tonight?"

"It's coffee." Jasper straightened his suit coat though it was already perfectly perpendicular. "Does that count as a date?"

"You just said it was a date," Lawrence said as Fisher popped the top on a diet cola and joined them. "Before you know it, you'll be flying to Belgium to pick out one of your own diamonds for a woman, just like Fisher and Marshall."

"And Tyler," Fisher said, though the man wasn't engaged. A fake engagement hardly counted, but Jasper knew the circle of people who knew about Tyler's fake fiancée was small, and apparently, didn't include Lawrence.

Jasper expected Tyler to walk through the door at that moment, but he didn't. "Is he coming tonight?" he asked.

"I doubt it." Fisher watched the door too. "He's pretty

broken up about Tawny. We'll have to get over there soon to make sure he's still alive."

Jasper nodded, wondering if starting something with the gorgeous Sasha was such a good idea. After all, Tyler had had his heart carved out by the first woman he'd dated since coming to the island.

Who's to say that wouldn't happen to Jasper too?

———

He arrived at Roasted with fifteen seconds to spare, if his expensive German watch really did adjust to the international clock the way he'd been told. The place wasn't terribly busy at eight o'clock on Tuesday evening, but he couldn't see Sasha anywhere.

She'd said she'd have to check with her staff and that she could only get away for an hour. He wondered what she did that required her to work in the evenings, and he was reminded how little he knew about her.

He unbuttoned his suit jacket and sat at a table facing the door, ready to wait. He'd never felt a great pull to be buddies with people. They could do their jobs, and he'd do his. Jacqueline was friendly, but he wouldn't classify them as friends.

And he certainly didn't want to put Sasha in the friends category when he saw her sweep into the coffee shop, her reddish blonde hair flowing behind her. She was tall, toned, and tan, and he wanted to kiss her more than he wanted to keep breathing.

Which was *absolutely* ridiculous. He needed to find out

a lot more about her before he even entertained those kinds of fantasies. He'd made that mistake in the past too —in fact, he'd come to Hawaii to try to rectify falling in love too fast with a certain brunette in Denmark.

He rose, a smile pulling at his mouth. She spotted him and came over, wiping her hands down the front of her shorts. "Sorry I'm late. We got hit with a rush."

"Oh, I've been here five minutes." He gestured to the chair opposite of where he'd been sitting, but she pointed to the back of the shop.

"Do you want to get some coffee?"

Coffee. Yes. Yes, they were here to get coffee. A furious heat hit him in the chest and he said, "Yeah, of course," in an even voice. Thankfully.

He let her go first and she ordered some concoction he'd never be able to remember or replicate. He wasn't even sure what it was, but he said, "I'll have the same," and stepped halfway in front of her to pay.

"I got it," he said, pulling a bill from his wallet. He handed it to the cashier amidst Sasha's protests. He twisted toward her and said, "It's our first date. Are you going to argue with me about paying?" He felt flirty and brave, and he was beyond pleased to see the sparkle in her eyes too.

"Our first date?"

"I sure hope so." *The first of many*, he wanted to add, but he bit back the traitorous words.

"Then I want a blueberry muffin too," she said, nodding to the girl behind the counter.

"Yeah. Blueberry muffin," he said.

"It's not a date if there's not food." Sasha lifted and lowered her eyebrows, all in a single heartbeat.

"Noted." He looked at the cashier, who held out his change, and said, "Put that in the tip jar," before he nudged Sasha down the counter so they could collect their coffees.

She picked up her cup and took a sip, and he copied her, getting a strong dose of vanilla and caramel but not a hint of coffee. He coughed, not expecting that flavor combination at all.

Sasha's twinkly eyes landed on him. "What did you get?"

"Same as you." He cleared his throat, trying to work up the gumption to take another drink.

"Do you even know what it is?"

"No idea."

She tipped her head back and laughed, and Jasper smiled at the happiness in the sound. He wanted to make her laugh like that every time he saw her. So he followed her back to the table where he'd been sitting, and she wrapped all ten fingers around her cup.

"So, tell me where you work," he said. "You got slammed? Must be a restaurant or something."

"I own The Straw," she said, searching his face.

"Oh," he said. "I know it. The drink place in the east bay."

"Right." Something shuttered over her eyes for a moment, and then she came alive again. She didn't give him anything to work with, so he flailed for another topic.

"Do you like it?" he asked, sticking with the same one while he searched for another.

"I love it." A closed-mouth smile accompanied the statement. "What do you do?"

He opened his mouth to say, but promptly shut it again. "I work with people overseas. Europe, mostly."

She watched him for a moment past comfortable, then switched her gaze to someone or something behind him. "Doing what?"

"Diamonds," he said. "I work in the diamond business."

"Oh, are you a jeweler?"

That would've been a much simpler life. He shook his head. "Sadly, no."

"Then what?"

"Why does it matter?"

She picked a sugared piece of her muffin top off and popped it into her mouth. Jasper stared, mesmerized by the movement of her mouth.

"Because," she said. "Jasper Rosequist, man with a home theater in his basement. You just paid for two cups of coffee—one of which you won't drink—and a blueberry muffin with a hundred dollar bill."

"Did I?" He hadn't even looked at the bill. Jasper did watch her, so he saw the pucker against her mouth, like she'd just tasted something sour. He watched the displeasure sweep over her before she erased it from her eyes. He saw everything, and it looked very much like this might be their last date.

"Well, I'll have to be more careful next time."

"You realize I can search for you on the Internet, right?" She lifted her phone.

"What's the fun in that?"

A smile touched her lips and she shook her head. At least she set down her phone without even swiping it on.

"I'll make you a deal," he said.

Her head shakes became more violent. "Oh, no. I'm done making deals."

It was his turn to lift his eyebrows, sensing a story. "What does that mean?"

She waved him away and took another bite of her muffin top. "Nothing."

"Can I propose my deal?"

She swallowed and sipped. "If you must."

"I must," he said in a proper British accent. Hey, it brought back the smile, and that encouraged him to continue. "I'd like you to come to the party I'm having this weekend."

FIVE

SASHA STARED AT JASPER. Tall, blond, annoyingly handsome Jasper. He did more than "work in the diamond business," and they both knew it. He wore a power suit to get coffee at eight PM, for crying out loud.

"I'm sorry." She shook her head, seemingly the only thing she could do tonight. "Did you just ask me to a party? At your house? That I clean?"

If only that was the bet Esther had tasked her with.

"Well, so far, you're the only guest." He ducked his head, his short, spiky hair doing nothing to cover the adorable blush staining his cheeks. Could he really like her? Could he be *interested*?

Why wouldn't he be?

Memories washed over Sasha so quickly, she became disoriented. Couldn't find her way back to the surface, and when she finally managed to, she sucked in a big breath as if she'd been underwater for far too long.

"You okay?" he asked, the blush gone. How long had she been freaking out?

She nodded and pressed her lips together. "Will you be inviting other people to the party?"

"I haven't decided yet."

She narrowed her eyes, trying to figure him out. "What would help you decide?"

"If I knew if you were coming." He smirked at her, and she actually liked his brazen approach.

"Depends," she said. "Weekends are pretty busy at The Straw."

"Do you work there full time?"

"Twelve hours a day."

"And you clean for me." He didn't phrase it as a question, but it burned in his forest-green eyes instead.

Her retort got stuck in her throat. She tried to clear it away, but only succeeded in making herself sound like she was dying a slow death.

Jasper nudged his coffee toward her, but she still had plenty of her own.

She got her coughing to stop and took a deep breath. "I've, uh, had some unexpected expenses lately," she said. He didn't need to know more than that. Didn't need to know she'd listened to the wrong person, implemented changes that had cost her a fortune to do and then more to reverse.

She blinked and his fairer features turned dark for a moment. When he spoke, it was with a foreign accent—and not a funny British one.

"...I'm sorry." He looked genuinely sorry, and thankfully like Jasper again instead of her ex-fiancé Newton.

"I'm recovering," she said.

"We all have to do that from time to time."

Surely he didn't, but Sasha didn't press the point. "So before I decide if I can come to the party, I think I should know a bit more about you," she said. "Any crazy ex-girlfriends out there?"

———

The next morning, Sasha didn't see or hear from Jasper. She felt like the walking dead, and she had to re-sweep the front steps three times before she was sure she'd done it. Not only was her mind whirring over last night's coffee outing—it wasn't really a date—but she couldn't seem to get her drink ideas out of her head either.

At least those hadn't abandoned her when Newton had, taking her entire staff with him. Of course, if he hadn't been cheating with her full-time employee, Sasha might still have Amber's help. Last she'd heard, Newt and Amber were somewhere in Europe, probably on one of those river cruises Sasha had talked to Newton about so often.

Sasha was just starting to get her mojo back after almost a year of heartbreak. She liked to have a new, limited-time specialty drink each month. They brought repeat customers who wanted something new, and she usually made a bundle on them.

She felt like her taste buds had abandoned her when Newton had, and she hadn't done a new concoction in six months.

So it was time, especially with Valentine's Day just around the corner. After all, she paid for the texting options on her loyalty account, and all she had to do was log in and send one message to get hundreds of people coming to The Straw over the course of a few days.

While she steam mopped the kitchen, she let her tongue direct her mind on which flavors to try for Valentine's Day. Something red or pink, for sure. Strawberries were the obvious choice. They were sweet, the right color, and ninety-nine percent of the population liked them.

But she had half a dozen drinks featuring strawberries. No, she wanted something more unique. More romantic. Something people couldn't get at Two Coconuts.

In fact, if she could figure out how to get more people over to the east bay, she wanted to do that. Maybe with her brain starting to function again after its hiatus, something would come.

Because of her repeated chores and distracted thoughts, she didn't have time to shower before heading to The Straw. She served customers, prepped fruit for the day, and kept everything clean. When Maddy showed up, Sasha let her take over the front of the stand while she slipped into the background to make the drinks.

In between customers, she made sample drinks, hoping to find the one that would be her Valentine's Day special.

Mango was a big favorite on the island, and it paired

well most berries and bananas. But it was too ordinary, and Sasha wanted something beyond that.

She tapped her pencil against the paper in front of her where she'd crossed out several ideas and fruit combinations already.

It was Valentine's Day. She needed sweet, romantic, pink…. "Passion fruit," she said, the words a little louder than she intended. But it was perfect, and right there in the name was everything she needed.

She scrawled the word in her notebook and followed it up with some possible drink names. *Passion fruit Power. The Power of Passion. The Passionate Pear.*

She liked the word play of the last one, but she wasn't sure pears and passion fruit would be the best pairing. The name would come, and what she needed to do now was find the right combination of flavors to go with it. She didn't currently have any passion fruit in the stand either, so she started making an ingredient list.

Ginger—she knew that went well with passion fruit. It would also bring a spiciness to the drink that would need a powerful sweet to overcome it.

"Peach," she muttered, jotting down one of her favorite fruits. Frozen peaches brought great body to frozen drinks too, and peach was sometimes a term of endearment.

Be a Peach. She added the name to her list, her mind whirring now. Coconut would make the drink tropical, and she eyed the bottle of syrup on her counter. It would take a delicate hand to make sure the exact right amount of the extract got added to the drink, otherwise it could be a flavor disaster.

Maddy called an order back, and Sasha left her notebook open on the counter as she got the desired drink blending. Business picked up then, and it didn't take long for Sasha to notice that a lot of the people getting drinks were wearing business attire.

"Where are you guys from?" she asked.

"The optometrist conference," one man said. "The line at the other drink stand was simply too long, and we were directed down here."

Sasha marveled at the number of men and women still streaming down the walkway under the palm trees. How long was the line at Two Coconuts? And would they bypass The Straw if she couldn't get drinks out fast enough?

"Send 'em all back," she said to Maddy, taking three new tickets. Sasha had six blenders, and no one knew her fruit combinations better than her. She worked at a feverish pace, determined to show these customers that the walk had been worth it.

Forty minutes later, the line had died and the beach in the east bay was dotted with people soaking in the Hawaii sun. Sasha watched them for a moment, feeling sticky from head to toe. She had approximately ten minutes to wash up and replenish her stock before the high schoolers would get out—creating another mini-rush that usually lasted about twenty minutes.

Amidst all of them, a sandy-haired man joined the line. Sasha's heart tumbled around in her chest like clothes in a dryer, but after another second of staring, she realized it wasn't Jasper.

It wasn't Newton either, though he'd stopped by her drink stand all the time while they were dating. *He doesn't even live here anymore,* she told herself as she turned away to make the next drink order.

But this man definitely wasn't there just to get The Guava Great.

"He wants to talk to you," Maddy said, stepping to the back of the stand and taking over the Purple People-Eater Sasha was about to cup up.

Sasha didn't turn around and didn't relinquish her hold on the blender either. "Who is he?"

"He didn't say. Looks a little shifty."

Sasha finished the drink, her empty stomach cramping as she turned to deliver it to the customer while Maddy started on the next ticket.

"How can I help you?" she asked, staring right into the man's dark eyes. Something predatory lived there, but she refused to look away.

"I'm Walter Cromwell," he said, his voice greasy. "You opened a Lettuce account several months ago."

She shook her head. "I didn't use any of that money." Another of Newton's great ideas—more credit than the bank down the street would give her. Apparently, anyone could get money online, and she'd filled out the application and been approved before Newton had pressed someone else against the door of the drink stand and kissed them—oh and then he'd skipped town.

Walter gave her what was probably supposed to be a sympathetic look. "Well, I'm afraid that's not true." He brandished a fistful of papers and laid them on the counter. "There's over a thousand dollars here that needs to be repaid, and we haven't received a payment from you yet."

Sasha's throat closed. "A thousand dollars?" She shook her head. "I didn't use any of that money." The papers felt like lead weights in her hands as she scanned the statement. "These aren't my charges."

"Well, they were made on your account, so…." That slimy, not-sympathetic smile again.

"I need to dispute them then," she said, her anger rising. She glanced at the several customers still in line and motioned for him to step around the side of the shack. He did, and she pushed through the back door with a look from Maddy that said *Hurry up!*

If only Maddy knew how much Sasha wanted to do exactly that.

She handed the papers back and said, "Look, those are airplane tickets to Spain. I didn't go to Spain in March last year." But she knew who did. "You can see my passport if you want. I haven't left Hawaii in years." The words almost choked her, but she drew herself up to her full height.

"It might be my account, but I didn't make those charges. I want to dispute them."

"Well, we don't really—"

"I'll give you the name and number of who did make them, and you can go after him for your money." She really didn't want to hear this guy start another sentence with "Well…."

And she wasn't paying for Newton's and Amber's little tryst to *Espania*.

Oh, no, she was not.

SIX

JASPER DIDN'T SEE Sasha on Wednesday or Thursday, and that was simply not okay with him. So while he was bone weary from a long week of cleaning up a mess he'd thought was irreversible, he set an alarm for ten o'clock on Friday morning. He was done working until Sunday night, so he could catch a nap later.

He deliberately didn't leave her money on the table with the list of chores either. When she'd admitted she worked twelve hours a day at The Straw and had some unexpected expenses, he knew she wouldn't leave that day without getting paid.

He tucked the five crisp hundred-dollar bills in an envelope and sealed it. She'd definitely come looking for this, even if he didn't catch her before she got in the shower. Satisfied with his plan, he got in bed and motioned for Frankie to join him. The forty-pound goldendoodle jumped up, his tongue hanging out of his mouth as he circled and then practically laid right on top of Jasper.

"Move over, bud," he told the dog, but Frankie just swung his head back as if to say, *What? This isn't okay with you?*

Jasper chuckled and gave the dog an affectionate pat. So maybe he didn't have a lot of parties or very many friends over to his place. But Frankie didn't seem to mind.

Turned out he didn't need his alarm, because he couldn't sleep. His thoughts kept rotating and tormenting him with thoughts of Sasha and if she'd arrived yet. What she'd be wearing that day. If she'd quit once she didn't need his money anymore.

Of course she will, he told himself. No one would voluntarily work seventeen hours a day if they didn't need to.

Jasper simply felt alive in a way he never had before, and that made sleeping difficult. When Sasha had asked him about his crazy ex-girlfriends, he'd had nothing to say. His relationships were always made of vanilla. If the fuse was there, it was short and fizzled out quickly.

As he lay in bed, he acknowledged the fact that he was lonely. So very lonely, especially after having Brighton and her kids with him for the holidays. The house had quieted considerably since their departure and he didn't like it.

Giving up on sleep entirely, he rolled over and picked up his phone. It would be late in Paris, but Brighton would answer his call, day or night.

Sure enough, she said, "Hey, brother of mine," almost as soon as the line started ringing. "Miss us already?"

More than she knew. Jasper chuckled instead, and said,

"I got a maid to do that deep clean." He laid back against his pillow, his eyes tracing the lines in the ceiling above him.

"Yeah?"

"Yeah." He exhaled. "I gotta say, though. I don't think that's what my house needs."

"Your house needs a deep cleaning," she assured him. "It also needs…."

"You can say it." He was already thinking it.

"You need someone, Jasper. How do you stand living there all alone?"

The despair welled behind his lungs at her words. Why did she have to be so dang good at saying the truth? He reached over and patted his chocolate-colored dog. "I have Frankie."

"It's not the same."

"I'm…working on that," he said.

"Oh?" Brighton sounded truly surprised. "You're dating someone?"

"Kind of," he hedged. "We went out for coffee once, and I invited her to a party, but she didn't ever say if she'd come or not." And he still hadn't invited anyone else. If Sasha said she'd come, he wanted it to just be the two of them, cuddled up together on the luxury leather couches in his basement. He wondered if she liked action films or more of the romantic comedy variety. He added it to his mental list of conversation topics.

Brighton laughed. "Coffee doesn't sound like a date. And you failed to get another one."

"She had a blueberry muffin too," he said. "And I have

her number." He wasn't going to admit to his sister that he had Sasha's number because she cleaned for him. Because he'd hired her over the phone, sight unseen. His heart jumped over a beat and then came back to it when he thought of her in one of the rooms below him, scrubbing or polishing.

"You got her number. Good man." Brighton wore a smile in her voice. "So did you just call to brag about your new semi-girlfriend?"

"No," he said quickly, though he didn't really have another reason. Maybe because Brighton was his closest human contact at the moment. "Just seeing if you're adjusting to real life after such a fantastic holiday."

She trilled out another laugh, which caused Jasper to smile. "We're doing great. The girls want to come to the warm beach again though."

"Anytime," he said.

"I heard you were coming to Europe?"

Jasper sat up, his grin gone. "Who said that?"

"Danni."

The middle sister.

"I don't know why she'd think that," Jasper said, his tone guarded now. He'd cleaned up the issue with the Swiss taxes. There was no reason for his father to get involved. But if Danni was saying Jasper was coming to Europe, then his father knew of the issues Jasper had spent hours on the phone dealing with.

"She just mentioned it this morning."

"Well, I wish." He blew out his breath. "All right, I was just calling to chat, but it's late there. I'll let you go."

"You sure?"

"Of course I'm sure."

"All right," Brighton said, clearly not believing him. "Hey, be nice to this woman. It sounds like you like her."

Jasper was about to say goodbye and hang up, but he stalled. "What does that mean? How can you tell I like her?"

"Jasper, you didn't even tell me about Lara until you'd been dating for six months."

"So?"

"So, you just called about a woman you've had coffee and a blueberry muffin with. Once."

He still didn't see her point, but it didn't matter. The clock was ticking closer and closer to ten, and he couldn't go another day without seeing Sasha.

"So be nice," Brighton said again. "Be charming. Be fun. Be all those things you are but don't show anyone."

"I show people."

"Did you wear a suit to the coffee house?"

Jasper grunted and sighed. "I had a meeting right before our date."

"*Riiight,*" Bright said, drawing the word out. "A meeting, when all your business is conducted overseas, over phone lines, Internet cables, and in the middle of the night."

"I have friends here," he said.

"That you wear a suit to meet with?"

"Yes," he said simply. Fisher had never set a dress code for the Nine-0 meetings, and Tyler certainly wore whatever he wanted, but Jasper had always worn his suits. He didn't get much opportunity to do so otherwise.

Working from home wasn't as glamorous as people thought it was.

"Okay," Brighton said.

"I need to go." Jasper swung his legs over the side of the bed, which caused Frankie to perk up. Sometimes he felt bad for the dog, like maybe he should give him to Tyler, who took his golden retriever to the beach every day. Frankie would love to romp through the sand and chase a Frisbee, but Jasper only took him every once in a while. And in the winter, it was usually dark, his favorite time of day to overlook the bay.

"All right. Be nice!" Brighton hung up and Jasper shook his head at his sister. What made her think he wouldn't be nice? Did she think he hadn't been nice enough to Lara and that was why things hadn't worked out between them?

He'd been nothing but nice to Lexie—and that was all. There had to be an element of wanting to be naughty with a woman to keep Jasper interested, and there was simply nothing naughty about a mutual fund heiress—at least not for him.

Now a broke drink stand owner in a tropical location... that was interesting, and Sasha definitely had his pulse pounding before he even left the bedroom.

He'd given her tasks on the patio today, as well as the pool house, so he loitered near the back French doors, wondering if she'd come in yet. When his alarm went off, he startled and silenced it, glancing around like he'd done something wrong in his own house.

Don't be a stalker, don't be a stalker, he coached himself. But he still moved away from the doors and toward the bathroom where she'd been showering. It was empty. So she hadn't come in yet. His investigative skills would surely impress the likes of Sherlock. He rolled his eyes and turned back toward the French doors.

"Hey." Sasha had just come in, and he startled again. She laughed and dusted her hands off. "Sorry to sneak up on you."

"It's fine," he said. "I was just looking for you."

"Oh yeah?" She had streaks of mud across her forehead where she'd obviously wiped her dirty fingers, and dang if the thought of her washing them off in the shower didn't have him sweating the way she was.

"Yeah." He thrust the envelope toward her. "It's Friday. Payday."

That beautiful smile lit her whole face as she took the money. "Great. Thanks." She wore another set of athletic clothes, this time revealing a little more of her strong shoulders. She must really have to pulp her fruit by hand, because the slenderness of her arm was accented with muscles.

He swallowed and tore his eyes from the curves of her body beneath the black, white, and gray spandex. "I wanted—" He cut himself off, trying to find the calm, cool, level-headed man who did multi-million dollar diamond deals with some of the toughest businessmen in the world.

"I'm free for dinner tonight," he said much slower.

"And I'm wondering if you'd like to join me." He would not ask her about the party until later. He would not.

He employed some of his steel nerves as he patiently— or not-so-patiently—waited for her to respond. When she still didn't after several long seconds, he said, "No crazy ex-girlfriends, we've established that. My middle name is Jenkins. And I'm hopelessly addicted to those Spam rolls over at Mama Chu's." He grinned when she settled her weight on one foot and cocked that sexy hip.

"But I feel like a loser when I go there alone." He shrugged, wondering why he was still talking when she hadn't said a single word. "So, you know. I need a date."

"Or a friend to go with," she suggested.

He took a step closer to her, those honeyed eyes never leaving his. "No." He drew the word out and inched closer. So close he could take her hands in his. He took her left with his right, the dust and dirt on her skin somehow making her more attractive. She wasn't afraid to work, and he really liked that.

"Not as friends." He swallowed, his point clearly made by now. "This would be date number two."

"Oh, you're keeping track?"

"You aren't?" Jasper's eyebrows went up and he leaned closer, his mouth mere inches from hers when he said, "I'm sure someone like you has rules for when a man can kiss her."

"Someone like me?" Her voice was definitely breathless, but her eyes blazed at him.

"Someone as pretty as you," he amended. "Someone who owns their own business. Someone who works as hard as you do. You don't just go around kissing everyone."

"No, I don't."

Jasper really wanted to kiss her right now, but he didn't want their first kiss to happen just inside the doorway of his house while he wore the closest thing he owned to pajamas. So he fell back another step. "So another date. Tonight. You tell me what time, and I'll pick you up."

SEVEN

JASPER SOUNDED SO sure of himself. *So another date. You tell me what time, and I'll pick you up.* Like he knew she'd say yes. Like he knew she was dying to say yes.

"It's impossible to know," she said instead.

"You don't ever take time off?" He watched her with those intoxicating eyes, and if she kept looking into them, she'd surely be drunk in the next moment.

"I only employ two people. It's hard to run the stand by yourself."

"So you need someone to help?"

"There isn't someone else." Disappointment cut through her. She wanted to go out with him again, this time for a real meal. A date where she hadn't changed in the back of her car outside the coffee house. One where she went home to her condo and showered—with hot water now that she'd collected on her bets and paid the electric bill—and curled her hair properly and put on that pink lip gloss Esther had gotten her for her birthday last fall.

"I can find someone," he said, the confidence and arrogance in his tone almost laughable.

"To run *my* stand?" She folded her arms, glad when it pushed her small chest up a bit. She'd never been too self-conscious about her body, but she'd seen Jasper looking at her with that hint of desire in his eyes. It lit something inside her on fire, and she wanted to make herself up and be as beautiful for him as he claimed her to already be. She knew she wasn't attractive with a sloppy ponytail on top of her head and sweat mixed with dirt all over her body.

"I know people who can take orders and make change," he said. "If your employee can handle all the drink making, you'll be set."

"Who is it?" she asked.

"I'm not sure yet," he said. "But I can find someone."

She squinted at him, still unsure. Just like she'd never confirmed nor denied if she'd be coming to the "party for one" tomorrow night, she wasn't sure she should accept or reject this date invitation.

"How about you text me who it is, and then I'll decide?"

He pulled out his phone and looked at it. "How about you shower and I'll find some help for you?"

She appraised him, but he steadfastly kept his attention on his phone, his thumbs flying over the surface.

Sasha retrieved her bag from where she'd left it on the bottom step and tucked the envelope inside. Once inside the safety of the bathroom, she allowed herself to open it and stare at the green, glorious money. "This job is definitely worth getting up early for," she told her reflection.

And the handsome billionaire paying her wasn't so bad either. She gazed into her own eyes. "Are you really going to go out with him?" So maybe things had started with a bet from her friends, and Sasha in desperate need of money.

No, she told herself. Something had started with Jasper the moment she'd laid eyes on him, framed right there in that bathroom doorway. Collecting on the bet was the easy part of the relationship.

Trying to figure out how she felt about getting involved with another wealthy man...now that was a whole twister puzzle she hadn't solved yet.

Not only that, but Stacey had texted not fifteen minutes ago with a new bet for Sasha. Only a hundred bucks to not only say yes to the party for one over the weekend, but to wear the black top she'd worn for Halloween a couple of years ago. When she was Catwoman.

It was a sleazy little thing, with satin over the breasts and mesh everywhere else. Sasha wasn't even sure she still owned it, but she was considering it because never had Stacey or Esther said she couldn't wear something over the top of it.

She wouldn't be wearing it alone, that was for sure. What would she even pair it with? Denim? She didn't need to come off as desperate or too forward.

Especially because you like this guy for real, she thought as she lathered up in the shower. The water looked like chocolate milk as it ran down the drain, and she'd never been so grateful for the modern conveniences of running water.

She took her time in the shower though it meant she'd have to rush through the prep at The Straw. When she finally opened the door, Jasper couldn't be found.

She considered searching for him, but she honestly didn't have time. Shouldering her bag, she started for the front door, settling on texting as her only option to discover if he'd found someone to work for her that evening.

"Trying to sneak off without saying goodbye?"

A yelp came from her throat, and she spun back toward the grand staircase. "Jasper." She pressed one hand over her heart as it thumped against her ribs. "You've really got to stop scaring me right after I shower."

He stroked his curly-haired dog and laughed, the sound full and lifting up to the two-story ceiling. He stood, and though he wore a plain gray T-shirt and a pair of athletic shorts, he was just as impressive as when he wore his midnight-colored suit. Maybe more impressive, because he seemed...real.

"I found someone." He grinned at her and extended his phone toward her, the dog standing too. She still didn't know its name. "Her name's Lexie, and she works for a friend of mine. Looking for some extra cash."

Sasha's heart sank. Of course she'd have to pay someone to take her place at The Straw.

"It's all worked out," he said, shaking the phone. "See for yourself."

"Jasper." She felt the excitement leaking out of her. "I...

well, I can't really afford to pay someone to work so I can go out."

"That's fine." He didn't miss a single beat. Didn't hesitate. "Because you're not paying her."

Accepting his charity would be worse, and she swallowed away the distasteful idea. "Well you're not paying them."

"Nope, I'm not."

She honestly didn't have time for this, but she couldn't get herself to leave. His back and forth, with the flirtatious tone and dreamy eyes, had her hooked. "Then how is this Lexie going to make some extra cash tonight?"

He moved forward and she fell back. He stepped, so did she, until she met the huge wooden door behind her.

He put one hand beside her head and pressed it into the door. "Leave it to me," he whispered.

"But that's exactly what I *don't* want to do." Her voice sounded at least an octave lower than it should. And he wasn't deaf. Surely he knew how he affected her. Did she cause ripples in his pulse too?

"I promise I won't pay her." He leaned down and pressed his cheek to hers. "Will you go out with me tonight? I found someone to take your place for a few hours."

Bathed in the masculine, woodsy scent of Jasper's skin, she couldn't say no. Didn't even want to. So she said, "Yeah, all right," hoping it wasn't the biggest mistake of her life.

———

Sasha giggled when Jasper knocked on her door later that evening. She'd left The Straw an hour ago and taken another hot shower, curled her hair like she'd wanted to, and currently wore that lip gloss. When she'd texted her club about her date tonight, the bet had morphed into *Kiss him.*

No way, she'd messaged back. She barely knew the guy, and she wasn't taking any more bets.

Kiss him! Kiss him! Kiss him!

Tawny's chanty texts rang through Sasha's head as she answered the door and stepped back. "Hey, there, handsome." She giggled again, and Jasper whistled as he scanned her from head to toe.

"Don't you look nice?" He smiled at her, and it was soft around the edges. Not the predatory kind most men wore when they looked at her. Jasper seemed genuinely interested and he was a perfect gentleman as he offered her his arm and added, "A bit dressed up for the Spam place."

He chuckled and she slid her arm into his. "Well, last time I changed into my clothes in the back of my car, so you get the dress tonight."

"I like it, don't get me wrong. But it feels like we should go somewhere a little more upscale."

"No, no." She shook her head. "You want the Spam rolls, and that's what we're getting." She liked Mama Chu's too. "Besides, they have these jumbo shrimp I *love.* Have you had those?"

"I never stray from the Spam rolls." He glanced at her. "So maybe you'd like to elaborate on any crazy ex-boyfriends I should know about."

Her heart stutter-stepped and she almost stumbled. "Nope." She popped the P. "No crazy exes."

"Hmm, I don't really buy that."

"Now, if you'd asked about a cheating ex. Yes, I have one of those. And he was a big fat liar too. And bad for me in just about every way, and I couldn't see it until he took my only full-time employee who he'd been kissing behind my back, used my money to buy them both a ticket to Spain, and left the island."

Jasper stopped walking, and humiliation filled Sasha. Why had she said all that? He would think she was the crazy one.

She gave a shaky laugh, hoping to cover up every issue she'd just exposed. "I mean—"

"I'm so sorry." Jasper kept her close and pressed his lips to her temple. "That must've been terrible. Is that why you have some unforeseen expenses right now?"

"One of the reasons." She didn't want to tell him about her own stupidity. How she'd followed Newton's advice instead of her own heart when it came to *her* drink stand. He didn't need evidence of her bitterness and her stupidity all on the same night.

"You still sound angry about it." He stepped again, slowly, toward the parking lot. His car wasn't hard to find, as most people who lived in these modest condos didn't drive gleaming silver sports cars with fancy foreign names.

"Yeah." She exhaled. "I mean, I am, and I'm not. I just found out about the ticket to Spain, so." She lifted one shoulder into a shrug, the strap of her tank top sliding down. "It brought back a lot of suppressed memories."

"Certainly you don't have to pay if you didn't approve the charges."

"I'm disputing them," she said. "I don't want to talk about it." She glanced at him. "Sorry. Um...family? Brothers? Sisters? Did you grow up here on the island?"

"No," he said. "I was born in the US but my parents moved to Denmark when I was five. I grew up there. Lived there for most of my life. I...had an experience with a woman in Copenhagen that convinced me to leave, and I came here."

Sasha wanted to know more about this "experience," but Jasper continued with, "My parents are retired now and living in Switzerland. My youngest sister—who's four years younger than me—lives in Paris with her husband and two girls. And Danni, my other sister is in Belgium."

"Wow, an international family."

"My father owns diamond mines all over the world." He opened the passenger door of his ritzy car.

Sasha paused and looked at him, a smirk riding her mouth. "Right. I think *you* own the diamond mines, Mister." She slid into the car, a laugh coming out of her mouth.

Jasper leaned down and asked, "Why do you think that?"

She looked up at him, imagining what it would be like to kiss him. She licked her lips and said, "Because you just said your parents are retired. So I'm sure you, as the oldest child, are running the diamond mines now."

"Oh, I don't run the mines." He flashed her a smile and went around the front of the car. She admired him in his more casual clothes tonight. Still date-worthy, he wore a pale yellow button-down shirt with short sleeves and perfectly pressed khaki pants. He was sinfully handsome, the light color of his shirt contrasting with the dark nature of his hair, the olive tones in his skin, and those foresty eyes that held something dangerous in their depths she wanted to dive in and explore.

"Of course you don't *run* the mines," she said when he got behind the wheel. How he fit his long legs inside was a mystery to her, even though she watched him do it. "You *own* the mines. My mistake."

"An easy one to make." He gave her another smile, not even denying that *he* now owned diamond mines all over the world. No wonder he was loaded.

"Tell me another mistake I've made," she said, enjoying this game.

"You don't even know my dog's name."

Sasha laughed, mindlessly reaching over and threading her fingers through his. He squeezed, and she realized what she'd done. But more happiness filled her than she'd experienced in the last four years, so she kept her hand in his.

"What's your dog's name?" she asked.

He slid her wicked grin and said, "Frankie," before pulling out into traffic and gunning the engine. She enjoyed the ride, especially because Jasper's car was so much nicer than Newton's. In fact, everything about Jasper was better than Newton, and some of Sasha's worries about getting involved with another wealthy man flew out the window as they drove across the island to Mama Chu's.

But she still wasn't going to kiss him. She glanced over at him, the joy on his face infectious, and her resolve to ignore the bet from her friends slipped a little.

EIGHT

JASPER OFTEN DROVE around the island at high speeds, usually with the roof down on his car. But it was almost always at night, with just Frankie beside him, when everyone else was asleep and only he could hear the waves against the distant shore.

That was an amazing rush, and one he took whenever his middle-of-the-night job got a little too stressful.

But this drive, with Sasha's hand in his and her laughter riding on the air, was a whole new kind of high Jasper wanted to repeat.

He pulled into Mama Chu's and parked before looking at her. He couldn't stop smiling, and the moment lengthened between them, this powerful push and pull of emotions raging inside him. Could she feel this magnetism too? Surely she could. It took two poles to attract.

She finally ducked her head, her silky hair falling between them. "Should we go in?"

"Yeah." He cleared his throat and delicately removed his fingers from hers. "Let's go in." He got out of the car and hurried around the front to open her door. Thankfully, she let him, and he took her hand again to help her stand from the low car.

"So shrimp, huh?" he asked as they approached the restaurant. It would be noisy and busy inside on a Friday night, the scent of fried food and soy already hanging in the air. But there were tables outside available, and he didn't mind the lively atmosphere.

"Do you not like seafood?" she asked.

"I love seafood." He opened the door and let her enter first.

"I like steak and shrimp," she admitted.

"Ah, surf and turf. A classic." The line wasn't too long, and it moved fast. He kept Sasha close to him though, and he wasn't at all sorry when he had to squeeze in to let someone pass by.

"So I've told you a little about my family," he said. "What about yours?"

She waved her hand, her eyes still on the menu, indicating she didn't come here as often as he did. "Oh, we're boring compared to Paris and Switzerland. Grew up right here on the island."

But her false nonchalance sent up a red flag with Jasper. "Brothers? Sisters?"

She tore her eyes from the menu—finally—and looked at him, vulnerability raging in her eyes. The silence emanating from her seemed to expand until it had enveloped them both in a bubble, and then someone said,

"Next in line, please."

Jasper moved, breaking the second tender moment between them, and ordered his Spam rolls and a side of sticky rice. "I think she wants the jumbo shrimp." He looked at Sasha, who had concealed her softer side in a matter of seconds.

"I do," she confirmed. "And the angus sliders with the Chinese slaw."

"Drinks?"

"Yeah." They both ordered a drink, and Jasper paid and took the number with him as he maneuvered toward the side door.

"Is outside okay?" he asked. "They have these big heaters."

"Sure." Sasha kept her hand in his as he led the way, and he wondered if he should just let the family issue drop. But it gnawed at him in the few minutes it took to get their table, fill their drinks, and get settled.

She looked down the street away from him, and he employed a bit of bravery. "So you don't have to tell me about your family if you don't want to," he said. "I didn't realize it was a sore subject."

Though now that he thought about it, why couldn't she call her mom or dad to help at The Straw in a pinch? Or with her unexpected finances? He really needed to give more thought to his questions before he asked them. But his family could've been a huge mess, and she'd asked.

"It's okay." She brought her gaze back to his and covered his hand with her other one. "My brother died when he was fourteen. He had leukemia." She nodded several times, little bursts of her head. "His name was Brian, and I started The Straw when I was only seventeen as a fundraiser for his treatments. I have a drink dedicated to him that I still donate all the proceeds to charity."

She released his hands and lifted her soda to her lips with slightly shaky fingers.

"Sasha." He liked saying her name, especially so quietly and with so much emotion. "I'm so sorry."

"It's okay," she said. "It was a long time ago."

"How long?"

She blew out her breath. "Let's see. I'm thirty-two now. He would've been twenty-seven in a few months." She put a smile on her face, but Jasper could tell it wasn't easy. "So he died thirteen years ago. My parents sold our house and moved over to Maui. It's quieter there, and they didn't have to face their neighbors or anything."

"And you stayed here and kept The Straw."

Challenge entered her expression. "I love my drink stand."

"I can tell. I didn't mean anything by it. I think it's great what you're doing, donating some money to charity." He grinned at her in what he hoped was a placating and passive way. Before he could say anything else, their food came, and he watched her face light up with the addition of steak and seafood.

"So I want to try a roll," she said, offering him one of her shrimp. "A trade?"

He pushed his plate toward her. "Take all you want." He had a feeling he'd give Sasha Redding whatever she wanted, and the thought both thrilled and terrified him.

They got the food they wanted, and she bit into the Spam roll without any hesitation, the act somehow increasing Jasper's attraction to her.

"Mm." She nodded as she chewed and swallowed. "That is good." She finished off the roll in a second bite, and he couldn't tear his eyes from her mouth.

Finally getting control of himself—it had been too long since he'd been on a date with a beautiful woman—he glanced down at his plate and picked up the shrimp she'd given him. The bite was crunchy and salty, with that beautiful savory shrimp flavor and he finished the jumbo delicacy before saying, "Yeah, I see why you like those."

"Right?" She practically beamed at him as she took a bite of her own shrimp.

"So what's your drink called?" he asked. "The one you named after your brother."

"The Cancer Killer," she said. "I was hoping it would be inspirational and all that, but...." She shrugged, a twinge of sadness entering her eyes again. "But it's got blackberries, raspberries, strawberries, goji berries, and oranges, so it really does have those cancer-fighting ingredients."

Jasper couldn't remember the last time he'd eaten a berry or an orange, but he kept that fact to himself. "I'd like to try it."

"Come on by anytime," she said. "In the winter, we're never that busy." Her face fell, and Jasper wondered if her finances were always strained, not just recently. He wasn't going to ask that, though. He had enough tact to keep his mouth shut.

"What about tonight?" he asked.

"Tonight?" Her eyes flew to his.

"After this. We can grab a drink and walk on the beach." It sounded romantic to him, but as the panic mounted in her eyes, she obviously didn't think so.

"Okay," she said at the same time he said, "We don't have to," with a shrug. He filled his mouth with an entire Spam roll, hoping to give her time to come back to her normal. He didn't like the wariness in her eyes, or the way she'd stiffened and still hadn't relaxed.

It took her two shrimp to release the tension, and he was dying to know why talking about something she loved—somewhere she spent twelve hours a day—made her so on-edge.

So he did.

"You're a brazen thing, aren't you?" Her eyes turned dark, but it wasn't all from displeasure. Her coy smirk made his internal temperature rise, and he could only shrug.

"You've seen where I work," he said.

"It's totally different."

"How?"

"I don't know. I just didn't know we'd be going there tonight."

"I can come by tomorrow then. I mean, it's a public beach and you do want to serve drinks, right?"

"Yes, of course."

"Then what's the problem?"

"It's just…." She heaved out a sigh and pushed the last slider toward the middle of her plate. "My stand isn't as nice as Two Coconuts. I mean, my drinks are way better, but Mo has a better location and a nicer stand."

"So what? You think I'm going to judge you?"

She nodded, her eyes half dangerous and half dancing with flirtation. "That's exactly what I think."

"What have I done to make you think that?"

She offered him the slider, and he indicated she should put it on his plate. "Oh, maybe because you're a freaking billionaire and well, I'm not."

"That sounds like a personal issue," he said, picking up the slider. "That has nothing to do with your stand." He took a bite of the slider, the juicy meat and garlic exploding in his mouth. "This is fantastic." He put the other half in his mouth and watched her. After swallowing, he said, "And I don't care how much money you have, or what your stand looks like, to be perfectly brazen, as you said."

That life that she'd somehow ignited blazed in him until she nodded.

"All right." He wiped his hands and mouth and tossed his napkin on the table. "I'm so thirsty. I really want one of those smoothies from The Straw." He stood and offered her his hand.

Sasha rolled her eyes and stood up too. "You don't have to yell it."

"They're so good," he practically bellowed, definitely drawing some attention from the other diners nearby.

She slipped her hand into his with a giggle, and Jasper felt content for the first time in years.

They arrived at The Straw a few minutes later, her nerves bleeding into the tiny sports car. Jasper got out and surveyed the beach, the stand, and the few tables around it. "This is great," he said.

"Two Coconuts does better," she said. "Because of that new hotel."

Jasper could definitely see that as being true. "Well, that's easy to fix," he said, glancing toward the other bay where he could definitely see the top of Sweet Breeze all lit up. "You just go talk to Fisher DuPont and ask him to feature your stand in his hotel." When he looked at Sasha again, she made a terrible scoffing noise and stomped away. Well, as stompy as she could get in sand.

"What?" he asked the empty beachwalk around him. He joined her in line at her own drink stand, not quite sure what he'd done wrong. Awkward silence reigned between them, but he'd been brazen enough for one night. If she wanted to talk, she'd have to start the conversation.

NINE

SASHA CLENCHED her arms around her middle, trying to keep her emotions dormant. But they swirled inside her like a whirlpool, becoming more violent the longer she stayed silent.

She did not need the advice of a freaking billionaire. He had *no idea* what running The Straw was like—he'd never even been to her drink stand before. He probably didn't even know what it was like to live in a house smaller than ten thousand square feet.

The storm brewed, billowed, grew, groaned inside her.

"Look," he said, and that broke her composure.

"No, you look." She turned toward him, very aware that she stood only a few feet away from her employees, and only a few inches away from other people. She grabbed onto his forearm and towed him further down the beach. They left behind the lights of The Straw until only moonlight fell over them.

Sasha felt sure she'd explode at any moment. "I don't need your advice."

"I wasn't giving you any advice." Jasper cinched his own arms across his chest, and darn him, it only made him seem bigger, more muscular, more impressive. "I *casually* mentioned you might want to talk to Fisher. I'm friends with him, you know."

"Oh, *of course* you are," she bit out sarcastically. "You and your billionaire best friends. What? Do you have a club or something?"

He blinked and in that single moment, she knew she'd hit the nail on the head. She sucked in a breath and covered her mouth. With wide eyes, she lowered her hand and said, "You do, don't you?"

Jasper gazed back at her coolly, his voice as equally unemotional when he said, "We're friends. We talk about business. It's not a *club*."

Oh, but it was. And Sasha would bet everything she'd ever made on her brother's drink sales that they had dinners and maybe even corporate retreats or something equally as fancy. Some of her anger ebbed away into the night, and this time when she crossed her arms, it was to keep the chill off her skin.

"Look," she said, this time with an accompanying sigh. "I...." Did she want to tell him this? Ninety percent of her did. The other ten percent was shrieking a warning about getting involved with another nosy, rich man.

He's not like Newton, she told that ten percent and it quieted.

"You've said 'look' twice now," he said, softening right

STRAW AND DIAMONDS   91

before her eyes. She liked this vulnerable side of him, the way he relaxed and let his emotions show in his eyes. Under the moonlight, they were still hard to read, especially as they raced across his face. "I don't want to fight with you. I just wanted to get a drink, hold your hand, talk about our lives."

Sasha heard the words he used, but she interpreted them a bit different. He wanted to *share* his life with her. The concept wasn't all that new to Sasha, but everyone besides her girlfriends in the Women's Beach Club seemed to have an agenda, like simply being her friend wasn't enough.

"I want that too." She bravely reached out and put her hand in his. "I may have overreacted."

"Why's that?" He strolled with her back to The Straw, which had a longer line now. Sasha wanted to be annoyed about that, but she simply couldn't be.

"My last boyfriend—the one who stole my money and went to Spain?—he had endless amounts of advice for me. Everything from what color the stand should be, to how big the drinks should be, to specials I should run."

"Mm."

Sasha appreciated that Jasper didn't rush to defend himself again, that he was willing to listen to her until she was finished. She wasn't sure when that had happened last. Her friends in the Beach Club were great, of course. But sometimes she felt overshadowed, or like she wasn't really being heard. The bets were an indication of that, and a prick of guilt that she'd done them and taken her friends' money stung her heart.

"Anyway." She shook away the feelings. Jasper didn't need to know about the bets, at least not right now. "I took some of his advice—all of it, actually. And a lot of it was bad, and I started losing money. I...stopped listening to my gut and my heart, and I'm still trying to rebuild from that."

And not just The Straw, she wanted to add, but the way Jasper's hand tightened on hers said he understood that her rebuilding process was about more than just her drink stand.

"Is that why you've had some unexpected expenses lately?" he asked.

"Yes." She stepped forward when it was their turn and smiled at Macey, who was handing a drink to another customer. "Hey, Mace. Two of Brian's Cancer Killers, large." She glanced at the woman taking the orders—the person Jasper had brought in.

"This is Lexie," he said. "She's a friend of mine."

The brunette beamed at Sasha like there was nowhere she'd rather be than taking orders and making change on a Friday night. "Nice to meet you. I see why Jasper was so desperate to go out with you tonight." She threw him a knowing grin, and he made a motion for her to *shut up!*

Sasha laughed, the sound of joy coming unexpectedly.

"Glad you think she's funny," he murmured in her ear, his lips so close, so close. She froze, the laughter dying in her throat.

"I assume there'll be no charge for the drinks?" Lexie asked.

"Oh, I'm paying." In one fluid motion, he withdrew his wallet from his back pocket. "How much?"

"Nine fifty-seven," Lexi said. She hadn't used the calculator on the counter. Or even looked away from Sasha yet. She seemed nice, like she enjoyed teasing Jasper, and that she knew him much better than Sasha did.

Jasper handed over a hundred dollar bill and said, "Keep the change."

Sasha started to protest, but his hand swept along her waist and pulled her close. "It's for charity, right?"

She nodded and said, "Right," but she wasn't sure if he meant for Brian's cancer research charity—or if Sasha herself was the charity case.

———

The next morning, Sasha finally got to sleep in. Jasper didn't require cleaning on the weekend, and she still hadn't said if she'd go to his theater party or not. They'd talked about a lot of things last night as they strolled through the sand, and Sasha wondered if she'd dreamed the whole date.

The empty cup with the dark purple dregs in it from Brian's Cancer Killer testified that she hadn't. So did the four texts waiting on her phone. All from Jasper, they wanted to know when he could see her again in some form or another without coming right out and saying it.

She smiled, a giggle slipping through her lips as she relaxed against the pillow again, the sunlight coming through the slats in the blinds.

So you're asking me out again, is that it? Date number three?

His response came in seconds. *Yes. When?*

She didn't mind that he was forward; she liked feeling like he was desperate to see her again. While she'd thought a lot about kissing him last night, the right moment hadn't presented itself. Even when he'd walked her to the door, something rippling between them that felt like electricity, the mood was still a bit awkward.

And while he was brazen and bold, he also had a vulnerable and hesitant side she really enjoyed. She'd swept her lips across his cheek and tiptoed through the door, closing it solidly behind her and drifting around the house until she made it to bed.

Is the "party" still happening tonight? She hoped it was, and that he hadn't invited anyone else.

Unfortunately, that has to be canceled. I have some family business I need to do tonight.

Her spirits fell, but Sasha understood family. She should probably go see her parents this weekend, and a plan to do exactly that formed in her mind as she thought about when she might be able to see Jasper again.

They both worked a lot in the evenings, and she didn't have a replacement. She didn't think his friend would want to fill in on a permanent basis, and Sasha wouldn't ask her to anyway.

I like to hike, she told him. *Maybe we could get away next weekend again? Do some hikes to waterfalls over at Oahu?*

She hadn't had time for hiking since Newt had taken Amber and left her high and dry to find and train new employees. Not to mention how she was still digging herself out of debt.

I can tolerate hiking, came Jasper's reply.

If you'd rather do something else, I'm all ears.

Several seconds passed while she fantasized about what he might say. He probably owned a yacht as big as the bay. Or a jet. Maybe he'd whisk her off to Paris for a night of tasting delicate pastries before he kissed her for the first time in the glow of the Eiffel Tower.

Her phone chimed, interrupting her insane imagination. He'd said, *A helicopter tour? Have you ever done one?*

Growing up in Hawaii, Sasha had always wanted to see her home state and islands from the sky. But her parents weren't wealthy—didn't own diamond mines across the world—and once Brian had been diagnosed, every spare penny went to his medical treatments.

So Sasha found herself at age thirty-two never having been on a helicopter tour of the islands. *Nope,* she texted. *Never been.*

Let's do that, he sent back. *I've always wanted to go and never made the time.*

Warmth flooded Sasha that he was making time to do more than work—and that it would be time he spent with her too.

Perfect. We'll be in touch. I think I'm going to catch a flight over to Maui for the weekend and visit my parents.

What about The Straw?

A groan filled her whole body. She couldn't believe she'd forgotten about it. And she hadn't. Not really. For some reason, she'd slipped back into the person she'd been before Newt had disrupted her life. A life where she had full-time employees to work some evenings and most weekends so she could have time off. A life where she could afford to pay those employees. A life where she wasn't working two jobs just to keep the electricity on.

She couldn't afford the plane ticket either. She didn't answer Jasper, the reality of her life a bit too heavy to carry at the moment. He didn't think about how much a flight cost or who would work for him. He had people to worry about those things, and they probably had people to take care of them.

But not Sasha. She had to take care of herself. As she dressed and started texting her mom, she wondered if perhaps she and Jasper were simply too different to have and maintain a meaningful relationship. Maybe he should just be her boss and she should just keep collecting his money in exchange for keeping his huge house on the hill free of dust.

TEN

JASPER EMPLOYED all of his will power to keep himself from hurrying over to the east bay and getting in line for a fruity, frozen drink. But he'd already come across as super-forward, and he didn't need to be perceived as desperate too.

Not only that, but the rain had decided to make a huge entrance that morning, and soon after Sasha went radio silent on their texts, the sky darkened and the bad weather rolled in.

With nothing to look forward to except an uncomfortable call with his father later that evening, Jasper felt like a caged tiger. He paced from the French doors at the back of the house to the front lobby where he left Sasha's cleaning list each day, Frankie right on his heels.

Jacqueline wouldn't be in today, and Jasper could literally spend all day cooped up in the house by himself. In fact, he had done that numerous times since buying the property and moving to Hawaii.

For some reason, today, he couldn't stand the thought. Sweet Breeze was busy on the weekends, and while Marshall usually wasn't, Jasper didn't feel like hanging out with the pineapple plantation owner and his girlfriend.

He wanted to be where Sasha was, but he once again told himself he would *not* be going to The Straw in the pouring rain. Maybe she wouldn't even open in this weather, and his thumbs twitched to get a text out and ask her.

Jasper exercised some self-control and set his phone in the charger so he could shower. Then he went down to the beach, but not to The Straw. To Tyler's. The man still hadn't responded since he'd broken up with Tawny Love- . less, the woman he'd started a fake relationship with only to fall for her for real.

Tyler didn't answer the door, but his dog barked. Frankie, who waited at Jasper's side, whined, and he said, "Go on."

The dog tore around the house, and more barking— none of it Frankie's came from the back yard, which went right up to the beach. Wet sand flew as the two dogs chased each other, and Jasper bent to pick up a ball before spotting Tyler lying in his hammock.

He lifted a lazy hand in Jasper's direction and let his head fall back toward the bay, one foot absently pushing the hammock every time he edged forward. The once-powerful poker player looked like a shell of himself, and Jasper's heart tapped out a warning.

If he continued things with Sasha, would he too end up with a broken heart and no reason to leave the house?

You already have no reason to leave the house, he thought as he took a seat at the picnic table, which thankfully had a umbrella over it, and watched the dogs. He had nothing to say—he knew better than most that words didn't always help—but he felt better just being in the presence of another human being.

"You should get that dog into agility training," Tyler finally said. He swung his legs over the side of the hammock and bent to pick up a Frisbee. He didn't seem to notice or care that water dripped down his shoulders from the palm fronds above.

"I sleep during the day," Jasper said, his voice almost a monotone. The rhythm of the waves pounding the shore a hundred yards away was calming and peaceful.

"What are you doing here?" Tyler ran his fingers along the edge of the Frisbee, probably waiting for one of the dogs to notice he'd picked it up. Frankie would go nuts—literally lose his mind—and Jasper once again thought he should hire someone to exercise his dog more often. Heck, Tyler would probably do it for free.

"Nothing," he said. "You have a hose, right? Because Frankie's already a mess." The curse of having a curly-haired dog was the clean-up if they got into anything at all.

"I have an outdoor shower." Tyler waved in the general direction of the house.

"Right."

"You still didn't say what you're doing here."

"I didn't—I—" It wasn't that Jasper didn't know. He simply didn't want to say it out loud, at least not to Tyler.

"Oh, wow. You too?"

"Me too?"

"I used to read people for a living," he said. "You're pining over a woman."

Jasper scoffed and tore his eyes from the undulating water. "Pining? I don't think so."

"What's her name?"

"Sasha Redding," slipped out before Jasper could censor it and change it to "No one."

"She owns The Straw."

"Right. Thanks for ignoring me last night." Jasper had literally texted everyone he knew for a favor the previous evening. That alone should tell him how much he already liked Sasha. And how much of a dangerous position he'd already put his heart in.

"You're welcome." He stood and slapped the Frisbee against his palm, which somehow echoed loud enough to get the attention of both dogs. Frankie looked like a chocolate streak as he barreled toward them. He was much faster than Lazy Bones, and he skidded to a stop in front of Tyler, his giant tongue hanging out the side of his mouth.

Tyler chuckled and bent to pat the dog. Clumps of sand went flying as Tyler scrubbed Frankie, and Jasper groaned again. That sand would be right up against Frankie's skin, trapped beneath all the curls. It would likely be hours before he could get his dog clean and go home.

Doesn't matter, he told himself. He didn't want to go home to his big, empty house anyway.

So he stayed until both dogs got tired of chasing the Frisbee, until the rain stopped, until he offered to go get dinner and bring it back since he knew Tyler didn't actually do a lot of cooking and liked to eat out every evening.

By the time he did get home, Frankie had been washed and dried, and darkness had fallen. He wanted to text Sasha, but she still hadn't answered his text that morning about who would run The Straw if she went to visit her parents.

Foolishness raced through him. Of course she didn't work twenty-four-seven. She surely had someone who could come in for her so she could take days off for family visits, relaxation, dates....

Maybe just not dates with him. He growled at the idea and tried not to read too much into it. After all, she'd held his hand and they'd had some great conversation last night once they'd gotten past that speed bump about the unsolicited advice she didn't want.

Still, he felt rather foul when his phone rang and it showed his father's face on the screen.

"Hey, Dad." He didn't mean to sigh as he said it, but somehow he did.

"Jasper." The man might be seventy-two years old now, but he'd lost none of his power and charisma, even half a world away. "Everything okay?"

"Absolutely fine, Dad. I told you that at least a dozen times this week."

"I know what's going on with the taxes," his dad said. "You still sound tired."

"I am tired." Working in the middle of the night was

tiring no matter how much sleep he got. It simply wasn't natural, and he wondered how much longer he could stay in Hawaii. Only three years away from turning the big four-oh, and he was starting to think life in Belgium would be much easier.

"All right. So I know *what* happened with the taxes," his dad said. "Tell me *why* it happened."

Jasper smothered another sigh as he opened his laptop and navigated to his email. He'd already sent the why earlier this week, and he decided he was just going to read what he'd already typed.

Then he could get back to thinking about Sasha.

———

Work started early on Monday, Tuesday, and Wednesday so that by the time he finished, he was so tired he could barely get himself into bed before passing out. He didn't see Sasha at all, but enjoyed their marathon texting sessions until suddenly she'd go silent.

He'd gone back though everything he'd said to see if he was accidentally pushing a button he didn't know about, the way he had with his suggestion to meet with Fisher. He couldn't find anything that would upset her.

He finally concluded that he was reading way too much into things. She was busy. Working seventeen hours a day, with only an hour or two off in the middle of the day—when he was asleep—to try to catch a nap.

She had started a conversation he wanted to finish, but

the time to bring it up didn't present itself on Thursday or Friday.

He read over her text again on Friday night when normal people slept. Already Saturday in Belgium and the rest of Europe, he had nothing to do but wasn't tired.

Do you think maybe we're too different? she'd asked at some point that week. He'd been asleep when the text came in, and there were several more following it that had kind of buried that initial question.

But it nagged at him. They did lead two very different lives, right down to when they slept. But he owned a business, and so did she. He liked dogs, and so did she. She'd told him more about her parents, what her childhood was like, and some of her favorite things.

That had been one of his favorite text strings.

A few of my favorite things, she'd messaged. Then she'd sent a clip of the song from The Sound of Music and followed it with items one at a time. His phone had chimed relentlessly for almost a full minute.

Tacos
Seafood
Shrimp (obviously)
Sunsets
Hawaii
Coffee with lots of cream
Dogs
The ocean
The Straw

The list went on and on. Jasper had started a list of his

own, but it was much shorter—eating out, surfing in the dark, his dog, and Spam rolls. He felt inadequate in his list, but she hadn't pushed him for more.

The conversation had moved onto surfing, something she'd never really gotten into. He'd offered to teach her, and she'd gone silent.

His phone had tormented him for six solid days, and he left it in the bedroom when he went downstairs to answer the doorbell. The pizza guy standing on the front step was easily as wide as Jasper and carried three boxes. "I've got a double pepperoni with olives, garlic bread, and cinnamon twists."

"Yep." Jasper held out a bill and the two men exchanged goods. "Keep the change. Thanks for driving up here."

"Anytime, bro." The huge Polynesian man grinned and turned to go down Jasper's steps.

Frankie sniffed the boxes and tried to jump up on Jasper as he walked into the kitchen. "Stop it," he told the dog. "You'll get some. When have I ever withheld pizza from you?"

Frankie sat, and sure enough, Jasper plucked a couple of rounds of pepperoni off the pie and gave them to the goldendoodle.

He managed to make it through a meal where he wasn't staring at a screen. Ants seemed to be marching through his bloodstream, and he took his last cinnamon twist upstairs with him to fetch his phone.

A green light blinked, which meant he had new texts.

Sasha had finally picked up their communication again, this time with, *We've slowed down and I can take off. Want to meet?*

The message was ten minutes old. He couldn't type *Yes* fast enough.

ELEVEN

SASHA SMELLED like lemons and ginger, and it was not all that pleasant. It was already ten o'clock, and Jasper had just responded that he wanted to meet. She didn't have time to go home and shower, so she scrubbed her hands in the sink at the back of the hut, hoping the industrial soap would be enough to rid her skin of the offending scent.

It had been a long, hard week. The rain seemed to be an angry spouse, always storming back into the room to punctuate their point with a massive downfall. The roof in her hut had been leaking all week, but she hadn't had time to fix it.

Because when it was sunny, there were customers. And when it was raining, she didn't want to get up on the roof and be a human lightning rod to find and fix the leak. She'd considered mentioning it to Jasper, who she suspected would send a team of people to have the leak fixed as soon as he knew about it.

Which was exactly why she didn't tell him.

She'd put her trust in one devilishly handsome rich man before, and she wasn't so sure she should do it again. But Jasper was so...nice. Newton would've shown up at The Straw the very first day he hadn't seen her.

At first, the extra attention was wonderful. Sasha felt like a princess, with the handsomest prince in the land trying to get her to pay attention to him.

Jasper was quite the opposite. He didn't come by The Straw, and he didn't even *ask* to come by. He didn't press her for another date. Didn't badger her when he asked questions and she didn't answer.

His aloofness was so endearing but also made her a bit nervous. So she couldn't wait to see him just so she'd know if he still liked her or not.

"Of course he does," she muttered to herself as she lifted her hands to her nose. She recoiled from the scent of gross pink soap, lemons, and ginger. That certainly hadn't been improved, and she'd have to keep her hands tucked in her pockets the whole time she was with Jasper.

"Knock, knock."

She spun at the masculine voice, surprised to see him already. How long had she been standing at the sink, daydreaming about him? She'd been caught doing it all week, actually, and Maddy had grilled her relentlessly until she'd spilled about the date last weekend, the hand-holding, the mini-fight about giving advice.

But there Jasper stood, just beyond the counter,

wearing a blue sweatshirt that had a big white C on the front of it. He smiled, and it lit up the entire beach.

She returned it and said, "Give me ten minutes to close. You got here fast."

He shrugged as if to say, *I like to drive fast*, and said, "What can I do to help?"

"Close that window. I'll put the fruit away." He lifted the awning and released the stick that held it up before letting it fall and latching it closed. His presence filled the whole shack when he came in the side door.

She fumbled the container of raspberries as she slid them in the fridge. Sasha faced him, her heart doing a weird tango in her chest that was quite painful. Or maybe she liked it. She wasn't sure.

"It's so good to see you," he said, nerves and vulnerability on his face though he spoke in that silky smooth voice. He entered her personal space in the next breath and wrapped her inside the circle of his arms.

She tried not to take a deep breath of his woodsy cologne, but she failed miserably.

"You smell great," he whispered, his hands tightening along her waist and keeping her right against him.

She laughed and put her arms on his shoulders. Oh, my. What strong, sturdy, beautiful shoulders he had. "I was just trying to wash off all the gross smells."

He gazed down at her, a softness in his expression that answered all of Sasha's questions about how he felt about her. "I like them."

She pushed against his chest, another giggle in her throat. "Come on," she said. "Let's get out of here."

"Where do you want to go?"

"I don't care. Just not in here." Because she thought she was going to kiss him, and she did not want to do that inside The Straw. She already had memories of her first kiss with Newt, almost in this exact spot, and she wanted something different with Jasper.

Because Jasper was different. Totally, one-hundred-percent different than anyone she'd ever dated before. And she had no idea what to do about that. She'd been wrestling with the decision to keep dating him all week, and she never could bring herself to send a text that ended their budding relationship.

He backed up, dropping his hands from her waist and capturing one of hers in his before he went back outside to the beach.

She paused and took a long, deep breath of the fresh ocean air. Her stand sat right on the beach—she had tables in the sand and everything—but somehow the walls kept all the freshness out.

"I love the bay," she said, squeezing his fingers.

"I do too." He gazed up at the sky, where the stars were already quite bright. With little light pollution in this bay, the night sky was magnificent. "I miss it when I have to leave."

She looked at him, finding some measure of homesick-ness in his face. But as she only had the light of the moon to see him, she couldn't be sure what he was really feeling.

"Do you travel a lot?" she asked.

"A fair bit." He focused on her. "I have to go to Switzer-land to take care of some business." A small smile accompanied the words, but he didn't seem like the same man tonight.

"You okay?" Feeling brazen herself, she reached up and ran her fingers down the side of his face. She might as well rent an airplane and write her feelings for him in the sky.

"I've missed you, that's all." This time, his smile brightened the night, and he tugged on her hand to get her walking. "Maybe we can just stroll the beach for a while?"

"Nothing I like better than strolling." She smiled and stepped through the sand, her shoes sinking in. "I need to take these off." She released his hand and removed her shoes, tossing them back toward The Straw, where they made clunking noises as they hit the wood. "I'll get them before I go home."

She re-laced her fingers through his and they started down the beach. Closer to the water, the sand turned wet, making it much easier to walk. "So," she said, another of her relentless thoughts surging forward in her mind. "I've been thinking about what you said."

"What did I say?" He spoke in a low voice, almost reverent, and the sound of it sent shivers along her shoulders.

"About talking to Fisher DuPont. You know, about doing something with The Straw."

"Oh, right." He flicked her a glance out of the corner of his eye. "So I didn't mess up too badly in suggesting it?"

Her defenses went right up, but she bit back anything she might have said. "No," she said slowly. "I maybe just needed some time to get used to the idea. I don't want to rush into things, not anymore."

He slid his hand around her waist and held her securely against his body. "I know." He pressed his lips to her temple, and she leaned into the touch. "I'll talk to Fisher. See when he's available."

"I was thinking—" She cut off, not wanting to be rude, not wanting him to think she was just using him. "Maybe I could have his contact information? Call him myself? I'll mention you, say it was your idea, all of that." She trusted Jasper; she did. He'd had a good idea, and she didn't want to dismiss it simply because it came from him and wasn't something she'd thought of.

But it had taken all week for her to get to that point, to work through everything. With Newt, she'd never done that, and it felt good to be listening to her heart and gut properly again.

"Do you want to go surfing in the morning?" he asked.

She almost tripped on the smooth sand and fell down. "Surfing?"

"I offered to teach you and you never responded."

"I don't have any gear."

"I'll bring everything you need." He somehow brought her closer, though Sasha felt the entire length of his body against hers with every step. "I usually go at night—about now, actually. But for your first time, it's probably best to go in the light."

The thought of surfing in the dark sent fear straight through her. "I'm not much of an ocean fan," she said.

"But you just said you loved the bay."

"I like the sight of it. I like the smell of it. I like laying on the sand in the sun. I don't actually get in the water that often. It…kind of freaks me out."

Jasper laughed, the sound happy but fading quickly. "Why?"

"I can't see under the surface. And there are *things* down there."

"Things," he repeated, a teasing quality in his voice she liked.

"Slimy things like seaweed and fish." She exaggerated a shiver.

He nudged her toward the water, and after several steps, the surf washed over her feet. Only an inch or two of water, and it was warmer than the sand she walked on.

Jasper slowed until he stopped, both of them standing in the gentle wash. "I love the ocean," he said. "The way it never gets tired of trying to come ashore. The sound of it, the smell, letting it push and pull me. It's very calming."

She listened to the water, breathed in the scent of it, and let the peace of it push and pull through her too. "I see what you mean."

He let out a long sigh that spoke of contentment, and said, "I'd very much like to kiss you now. Doable?"

Her heart stalled altogether, but a nervous giggle leaked from her lips.

"What?" he asked.

"Do you just say everything you're thinking?"

"Usually." He stepped in front of her and took both of her hands in his. "Is that a problem for you?"

She gazed up at him, the moon in front of her and casting his face in silver shadows. "Not really." She liked that he wasn't playing games. That she didn't have to try to figure out how he felt.

"I did want to talk to you about something you texted this week," he whispered.

But Sasha was already tipping up onto her toes for that kiss. "Can it wait?" Her lips touched his for one tiny moment, barely a heartbeat of time passed before she put an inch between them.

"Definitely." His breath wafted across her cheek and then he slid both hands around her and pulled her flush against him for a proper kiss. He was as brazen with the motion of his mouth against hers as he was with what he said, and Sasha didn't mind. Not one little bit.

TWELVE

JASPER COULDN'T BELIEVE his reality was kissing a beautiful woman while the surf lapped at his ankles. All kinds of things that had long been dormant were awakening inside him, and he didn't quite know how to grapple with them.

So he just kept kissing Sasha, the gesture becoming more fervent, faster, fiery, until he slowed the movement, turning it tender again.

He finally pulled away and tucked her against his chest while his pulse thundered in his chest. Neither of them said anything, and the moment burned in his mind, searing into his memory where he knew he'd never forget it.

"What about hiking tomorrow?" she whispered against his collarbone. "Instead of surfing. I need to work myself up to that."

"Is that why you didn't answer me when I offered to teach you?"

She took a few seconds before she answered. "I'm sure I just got busy. I don't remember specifically deciding to ignore you." She stepped back a foot and lifted her fingers to his hair. He thrilled as she moved them behind his ear and along the back of his neck. "What did you want to talk about?"

Jasper tore his eyes from hers, needing a moment to organize his thoughts after that heated kiss. "It was about...you said you thought maybe we were too different."

She started to move away again, but he held her in place close to him. "I...I thought about a lot of things this week."

"I can see that. I enjoy the texts." He smiled so she'd know he wasn't mad. Or even close to upset. They were just talking. He reminded himself that she'd come from a bad relationship and was still paying the price of it.

"I don't think we're that different," he said.

"You're rich. I'm not."

"So what?"

She shrugged. "It's just a difference."

"We both like dogs, and smoothies, and the bay. And pizza, and Spam rolls, and Mama Chu's, and—"

"All right." She laughed and tipped up to kiss him again. "I like kissing you."

"Another similarity." He grinned down at her. "And hiking. I like hiking."

"Me too." She started walking again, keeping her foot-

STRAW AND DIAMONDS   121

steps along the edge of the water. "But you do work all night, and I work all day. Makes it hard to have any time together. That was all I was thinking."

"I think we're managing okay." His looming trip to Switzerland flashed through his mind, but he kept it quiet. "Don't you?"

"Yes," she said. "I think we are."

———

Frankie pulled on the leash, and Jasper wanted to let him off. But the trail they hiked was a popular one and he and Sasha and Frankie weren't the only ones on it. The dog would have to deal with being tethered to him.

"I'll take him." Sasha paused and he passed the leash to her. Frankie seemed happier about that and he stayed right by her side.

Jasper shook his head. "Traitor," he muttered as they started hiking again. All around them, the lush tropical forests of Hawaii bloomed. Though it was only the beginning of February, everything was still green and beautiful.

He'd leave for Switzerland on Monday morning, after his usual business overseas. He rarely saw Sasha during the week, and he expected the trip to be so quick he'd be back by the weekend.

He took a breath of the hot, humid, floral air and enjoyed every moment it took for them to get to the Pe'epe'e Falls. They'd already seen Rainbow Falls, but they'd come too late in the morning to actually see the rainbows.

Not a lot of people continued on for the next mile and a half to the next falls, but Sasha had wanted to. Jasper didn't mind. It became less and less crowded as those who'd arrived in time for the rainbows that morning had already been to Pe'epe'e and were making their way back now.

The banyan trees were beautiful as was the Waikulu River. They finally arrived, and Jasper took his bottle of water out and took a long drink. There was quite a bit of water coming over the falls, and no one was swimming in the Boiling Pots, the swimming holes at the bottom of the falls.

In fact, at least half a dozen signs warned people from doing that. Sometimes, if the water was low, swimming was okay, but the pools weren't called Boiling Pots for no reason.

"Can he swim?" Sasha looked back at Jasper, her hand poised on the dog's leash.

"He'll probably be okay." Frankie was a champion swimmer, and he bounded into the water as soon as Sasha unclipped him. Jasper smiled at the goldendoodle's exuberance and he pulled out an apple and offered it to Sasha.

"We should've brought lunch." She perched on a rock and took a bite of the apple.

"I thought we were going to lunch."

She swallowed and smiled. "Yeah. I just like eating here, listening to the water for while."

"Well, we can stay as long as you want." He stretched his back and pulled out his own apple, keeping his eyes on

Frankie so the dog wouldn't go too far into the pools. It was peaceful at the falls, and after about ten minutes, they were alone.

"I'm going to Switzerland on Monday," he said. "I'll be back on Thursday night. Late."

She met his eyes. "Oh?"

"I just need to tend to a few family things." He wasn't particularly looking forward to it, though he did love seeing his mother. His father would ask him too many questions and demand he do things the way they'd always been done. But Jasper knew businesses didn't thrive that way. They had to change with the times, with the technology, with the trade, or they got left behind.

His father hadn't had to live through a period of great change, but Jasper was. Fisher's simulations for the storm about six months back proved that, and Jasper had been working with him on a robot that would help find diamonds below the Earth's surface without disturbing the environment with bulldozers and big holes.

"My father can be quite demanding," he admitted. "I love him, don't get me wrong. But...well, sometimes he still thinks he's in charge."

Sasha leaned against him and said, "My dad didn't want me to start The Straw. I did it anyway. I think he's still disappointed I didn't go to college, all these years later."

"I suppose most parents want big things for their kids."

"Yeah."

He enjoyed the weekend with her, especially their last kiss together, where he pressed her into the door of The

Straw, the scent of oranges and raspberries hanging the air, her hair, everywhere.

His nerves fired on all cylinders as he waited to board the plane on Monday morning, his mouth turning dry. Oh, how he hated flying, even as much as he'd done it over the years. It never got any easier, and he felt feverish and chilled at the same time as he had his e-ticket scanned on his phone and went down the jetway.

He had a seat in first class, but the extra width and longer leg room couldn't erase the fact that he'd be forty thousand feet in the air, above a huge body of water, for hours. Panic reared, and he worked to tamp it down by singing a childhood rhyme his mother had soothed him with.

As other passengers continued to stream past him, seemingly without a care in the world, he managed to switch out the song lyrics for thoughts of Sasha. He relived that last kiss and the several others they'd shared. A smile graced his face, and while he gripped the armrests on take-off, he managed to find sleep as he flew across the Atlantic Ocean to Europe.

Hours later, he finally got out of the taxi cab in front of the cottage his parents had purchased in Bern. The house looked like something out of a Swiss magazine, complete with the icicles dripping off the pitched roof.

He stood for a moment in the cold, the difference between Bern and Hawaii stark and freezing. At least Jasper had remembered to pack a coat, and he pulled it tighter around his throat as he moved toward the quaint front door his mother had painted red the second week after they'd moved into the cottage.

The front door opened before he could mount the few steps, and his father filled the doorway. "Joan, Jasper's here." He turned back to his son and smiled. "Come in, come in. It's freezing out here."

Jasper couldn't agree more, and he hastily stepped inside the house, which carried the scent of gingerbread as well as all the warmth in the world.

"Jasper." His mother appeared in the doorway that led to the kitchen, her face alight with joy. She brushed her hands on her apron and said, "How was the flight?"

"Horrible," he said, moving through the small front room that housed his mother's prized piano and a pair of recliners with a round table between them. "But I survived." Out of the billions of people on the earth, only his mother knew of his extreme fear of flying. Even his father didn't know, and Jasper wanted to keep that number at two.

His mother's arms came around him, and Jasper relaxed into the embrace. It had been months since he'd seen his parents in the flesh, and the scent of flour and fruity perfume filled his nose, so familiar and so comforting, Jasper was glad to have made the day-long trip halfway across the globe.

"Something smells good," he said, his stomach reminding him that he'd been too anxious to eat anything while he traveled. He needed a bit of that brazenness Sasha was always commenting on, especially if he was to deal with his father tonight.

"I made that chicken and wild rice soup you love," she said. "Come into the kitchen."

He went with her and found a tray of bread rolls rising on the small dining room table in the corner. "Mom, this all looks great."

And thankfully, his father allowed him to settle at the bar and chat with his mother until the bread was baked and the soup served. In fact, Jasper got the whole evening to just be, and he enjoyed it more than he'd thought he would.

When morning came, though, his dad already had several folder's worth of documents across the table where they'd eaten the night before.

"Morning, Dad." Jasper poured himself a cup of coffee, wondering how they got it to be so rich in Switzerland and sat in the vacant chair opposite his dad.

"Morning." His father looked over the top of his reading glasses. "How'd you sleep?"

"Well enough." Jasper had learned over the years that an answer of "well enough" got him through most conversations. He'd actually slept like the dead and woken with the thought of bringing Sasha to this picturesque country on their honeymoon.

Honeymoon.

That word had nearly sent him right back into a tailspin, and he couldn't live another day in the turmoil he endured when he had to fly. So he'd showered and taken a few extra minutes to shave before facing his father.

His mother had not asked if Jasper was dating, but he fully expected the question before he left. With both of his sisters already married, Jasper was definitely the late bloomer and odd man out.

"Well, these all look like they're in order," his father said, drawing Jasper away from the snow falling outside the window.

"I told you they were." Jasper lifted the mug to his lips and sipped, trying to keep his impatience out of his voice.

"I have someone I want you to meet with," his dad said.

"Who?" Jasper had spent more time in meetings than he cared to catalog, his general loathing for them rearing its head.

"Dominique Accola. She's an investment banker out of Zurich."

"I have bankers, Dad." Jasper set his coffee mug on the table and crossed his legs.

"I sent her these documents and she's agreed to help us."

"We don't need help." He glanced toward the mouth of the hallway that led to the two bedrooms, noting that his mother had not stirred yet that morning. "Where's Mom?"

"Oh, she likes to sleep in these days." His dad shuffled a few pages. "Dominique is expecting you at ten o'clock this morning."

Jasper gave an exaggerated sigh and met his father's eye. "Dad."

The older man wouldn't relent, as Jasper could see by the flint in his father's expression. "I just want her to educate you on the tax laws here."

"I have people who've already done that. It was not my fault the wrong paperwork was filed."

"Who's fault was it?" His dad's eyebrows cocked in an arrogant, annoying way.

"A box was simply left unchecked." Jasper stood, his appetite for coffee gone. He was sure Bern had much to offer in the way of delicious pastries, and he shrugged into his coat. "I'm going to go grab some breakfast. Want anything?"

"Ten o'clock," his father answered, and Jasper exited the house, wondering if Sasha would be busy at eight p.m. on a Tuesday night. He decided to dial her anyway, even if all he could do was listen to her voicemail.

THIRTEEN

SASHA TRIED NOT to think about Jasper every second of every day. Sometimes she succeeded, and sometimes she wondered if she'd put in the right amount of lemon zest or too much almond extract.

No drinks came back, so she figured she hadn't done too bad of a job. She wasn't cleaning for Jasper that week, and the extra time in bed had been so luxurious she'd considered quitting. But the money was easy, especially when she got to kiss him before she left.

He'd called and texted a few times, and his last one had said, *I'm going to stay for a couple of extra days. The weather is supposed to be bad here, and they'll cancel the flights anyway. Sorry, sweetheart.*

Sweetheart had burned itself into her retinas, and she could still see it there when she went to work on Friday morning. A drink—her brother's special—did come back, and that was when Sasha wiped her hands on a white towel and said, "I'll be back in a few minutes," to Maddy.

She stepped out of the shack and onto the beach, the sand warm though the sun wasn't particularly strong that day. She texted Stacey, Esther, Tawny, and Winnie, trying to keep the desperation out of the order of the words.

Jasper isn't coming back right away. Beach today?

Will he miss Valentine's Day? she wondered but refused to put in the text. Her friends would ask her anyway, and as her phone buzzed and beeped, she couldn't help smiling at their friendship and support.

They were all in, just waiting for her to name the time. They all knew what she'd been through over the course of this last year, and that she'd been working like a dog since Newt's departure from her life.

Three-thirty, she sent and then pulled up Macey's number to see if the girl could come in an hour early so Sasha could go meet her friends.

———

"There she is." Esther grinned at Sasha as she trudged through the last few yards of sand to where her friends had set up the Women's Beach Club. They were all there already, as she'd been hit with an after-school rush and had left The Straw fifteen minutes late.

"Sorry." She exhaled as she sank onto the sand. Exhaustion ran rampant through her muscles and bones despite being able to sleep in these past few days. Her eyes drifted closed, and the weak sunlight beat down on her, painting everything white and then red.

"Are you going to nap?" Tawny nudged her with a bare foot. "I have some news too."

Sasha opened her eyes and sat straight up. "Oh my gosh, you do. It's February tenth."

Tawny smiled and glanced around at the group of women.

"Did he read the article?" Sasha hated being left out, and she examined everyone's faces. She couldn't tell if they knew or not.

"You called this meeting," Tawny said, lifting her chin and speaking in a higher voice.

"Oh, come on," Stacey said. "We've heard nothing from either of you for so long. Someone start talking."

Sasha met Tawny's eyes, and said, "Might as well start with good news."

Her friend's eyebrows went up. "So that's me?"

"Is it?"

Several long seconds passed before Tawny's mouth curved upward. "All right, fine. Tyler saw the article, and we got back together." A squeal went up after her words, and Sasha couldn't help the flood of jealousy that rushed through her. Her throat narrowed but she smiled and told Tawny she was happy for her.

Which, of course, she was. Watching her these past several weeks had been painful, and Sasha was glad love could win out in the end. Of course, of all the women sitting on the beach, everyone seemed to have found exactly what they wanted—except her.

"So." Stacey popped the top on a can of soda, sending a clack-swish into the air. "You texted us today. Jasper isn't coming back?"

"He's coming back," Sasha said quickly. "But he was supposed to be home yesterday, and he's decided to stay through the weekend." She didn't want to say Valentine's Day, so she kept the words under her tongue.

"You must like him," Esther said. "To be worried about missing the most romantic day of the year with him."

"I didn't say...." She watched the waves and added, "Yeah, I really like him. He kissed me last weekend."

"Ooh," Stacey said with a giggle. She took another long swig of her soda, almost spitting it out when she said, "Oh." She coughed and set her can in the sand. "I was supposed to tell you to call Fisher. He can meet with you in the morning."

Sasha's spirits lifted enough for her to put a smile on her face. "That's great. Thanks, Stace." She'd called and left a message with Fisher, but it wasn't a surprise to get a message back through his fiancée. "I'll find out what time." She focused on her phone so she wouldn't have to vocalize any more of her concerns.

Of course, she should've known better, because as soon as she looked up from her device, she found all four pairs of eyes on her. "What?" she asked.

"He'll be back in time for Valentine's Day," Tawny said.

"He likes you as much as you like him," Esther added.

Sasha thought of the careful, controlled way he kissed her sometimes. The tender, gentle way he explored her mouth at other times. And the passionate, wild kisses they'd shared. She wasn't worried about him liking her; she felt certain he did.

But did he like her enough?

Newton had liked her too. But not as much as Amber. Not enough to stick around. Simply not enough.

And with Jasper as handsome as he was, and in a foreign country that he'd claimed to love several times this month, she wondered if she was a strong enough draw to get him to come back to Hawaii.

———

The next morning, she arrived at Sweet Breeze twenty minutes before her appointment with Fisher, nerves parading through her stomach. She wiped her palms down her slacks as she stood in the expansive lobby and reminded herself that she could do this.

She'd been kissing a billionaire, for crying out loud. This was just another man with a lot of money. She didn't want to kiss him, but somehow Fisher had an inexplicable power over her she didn't understand.

She turned, half the thought that she should leave and get back over to the east bay and get ready to open The Straw. A rack of brochures caught her attention, and she walked toward it. The slots at the top held full-size magazines, with the row beneath more typical-sized brochures.

The Spam Hut, The Roast, Two Coconuts, Mama Chu's....

There was no reason she couldn't have a brochure here too. She spun, her determination strengthened, and walked over to the check-in counter with certainty in her step. "I'm here to see Mister DuPont," she said to the well-dressed man standing at the corner. He wasn't a check-in attendant, and he wasn't all the way behind the counter.

He still sized her up for a moment, and Sasha was extremely glad she'd opted for the shiny heels and the blouse the color of ripe plums. "You must be Miss Redding," he said, his voice as smooth as silk.

"I am."

"I'm Owen Church, Mister DuPont's general manager. He's expecting you." He gestured her down the hall to the right of the counter.

She smiled and stepped past him, her shoes clicking against the expensive tile.

"The door there, on the left," he said, and she reached for the handle.

Fisher stood at a fish tank, his back to her, when she opened the door.

"Fisher," Owen said, and the other man turned. He extracted his hands from his pockets and beamed a bright smile at Sasha.

"Morning," he said. He was polished and poised, and Sasha could see why Stacey had fallen for him. "Stacey's told me so much about you." He crossed the room and shook her hand, holding on a bit too long. "Don't worry. Jasper will be home by Monday, I'm sure of it."

Unsure how to respond, Sasha sputtered. Thankfully, Fisher took a seat in one of the chairs in front of the desk while Owen navigated around it, and said, "So I understand you want to do some advertising here at Sweet Breeze."

"I was hoping for a trade," she said, sure advertising at Sweet Breeze would be astronomical in price. "I've seen the brochures downstairs for other local businesses, and I've seen cards and coupons for your restaurants, the movie theater, the aquarium, and your beach yoga classes at those local businesses." She drew in a big breath, prepared to continue. "Now, I know I'm over in the east bay, but there are plenty of people over there who need to eat, and who stay in hotels without the amenities you've got here."

She folded her hands in her lap and flicked a look in Owen's direction. The man stared at his computer, seemingly unaware of the conversation in front of him.

Fisher regarded her for maybe half a minute, but it felt like a lifetime to Sasha. "What do you think goes best with your drinks?"

Sasha hadn't been prepared for a question and answer session. "Well," she said, her brain whirring, trying to come up with an answer. "Pastries. A meal. Relaxation on the beach." She waved her hand like maybe more answers would fall out of the sky.

"But it's about a fifteen-minute walk from your drink stand to my bagelry, my restaurants, or the beach here." He steepled his fingers and looked at her, a challenge in his eyes.

"So we just need a reason for them to go back and forth. I can give half-off drinks to anyone who eats in your restaurants. You get full price food sales; I get more business over in the east bay." Sasha felt one breath away from complete shutdown, but somehow she kept breathing, kept thinking, kept gazing evenly back at Fisher.

She hadn't expected him to simply say, "What do you want? I'll do it for you," but she hadn't expected him to be quite so…closed to the idea. He obviously advertised for other businesses.

"Yours would be the closest movie theater," she said, seizing onto the idea. "And the aquarium, and the museum. I can advertise for those. The more people you have here, the more likely they'll be to eat or shop while they're here."

It felt like an eternity before a smile spread his lips. He simply said, "Owen," and the man slapped a button on the keyboard, which sent a printer whirring.

Seconds later, he stapled three pages together, and Fisher said, "My standard contract. Read it over and let me know if you have any questions."

Sasha's heart pounded beneath her ribs, and she forced herself to focus on the words on the page. Everything looked to be in order. Honestly, even if it wasn't, she needed her coupons or brochures in this hotel, where thousands of people stayed each week.

Her eyes caught on *Vendor will provide their own coupons or brochures, cards or other printed material, and it is Vendor's responsibility to check the stock of such items at Sweet Breeze.*

So she'd need to get some coupons made as soon as possible. "Got a pen?" she asked.

Owen held one out to her, and she signed her name,

exuberant and thrilled she'd done something to help increase business at The Straw.

"Thank you, sir," she said as she stood.

Fisher shook her hand and then reached for something Owen held toward him. "We're trying to increase our indoor activities during the winter months," he said. "I would love these to be given to each guest at The Straw who makes a purchase this week."

She took the cards from him, the professional quality of them beautiful and brilliant. "You have a bowling alley here?" She glanced up at him and then Owen.

Fisher merely smiled, and Sasha nodded before turning toward the door. With her hand on the knob, she twisted back. "Who printed these for you?" She lifted the cards a couple of inches.

After all, while she was here, she might as well get all the intel she could.

Fisher looked at Owen, who said, "Simone Agrippa, over at Paisley's."

"Thank you." She opened the door and stepped through it, surprised when Fisher came with her.

"I talked to Jasper this morning," he said. "He said to tell you hello."

Sasha's heartbeat played leapfrog with itself, and she couldn't help staring at Fisher. "He called you?"

"Oh, I called him." Fisher moved with the power and grace of someone who'd had to do so in front of a lot of cameras. "He sounded tired. His family has a way of wearing him out."

He'd never told her as much with those exact words,

but she'd gotten that idea too. "Should I call him?" She wanted to recall the words as soon as she'd said them, but Fisher didn't break stride or look as if she'd said anything too vulnerable or too needy.

He shrugged and said, "Depends on if you want him to know how you feel about him." He gave her a smile, and someone called his name, and he walked away.

Sasha watched him go, wondering how deep her feelings for Jasper were and if she cared if he knew or not.

She pulled her phone from her pocket, because there was only one person she wanted to share this marketing win with, and he was currently halfway across the world in Switzerland.

FOURTEEN

JASPER'S PHONE RANG, and he couldn't grab it fast enough. No, Dominique whisked it out of his grasp with that irritating smile he'd been enduring for three days. He'd thought he'd be meeting her at the bank, and he had.

But they hadn't been back there since. It was like Dominique had attached herself to him and she'd gone everywhere he had for seventy-two solid hours, even sleeping at the house like she was his parents' long-lost daughter.

His mother had been making comments about her beauty and his dad had dropped not-so-subtle hints that Dominique was single. Jasper had told his mother that he had a girlfriend on the island, but she'd developed selective hearing.

"We want you to come back to Europe," she'd said, like that meant it would happen.

"Mom, I live in Hawaii. I'm happy there." He loved his

parents, but all the reasons he'd left Europe a decade ago were like bright, neon signs.

In the end, since neither of his parents would listen to him, he'd decided to just let his time in Switzerland run out and get back on the airplane and get home as fast as possible.

"Ooh." Dominique's dark-eyed gaze came back to him. "Who's Sasha?"

Before he could answer, she opened the call with, "Jasper Rosequist's phone, Dominique speaking." She tacked a giggle onto the end of the sentence like they were fifteen-year-olds instead of business professionals.

He made a grab for the phone, but not before she pulled it away. "Yes, he's sitting right here with me. We're having dinner."

She made it sound like a date, and everything in Jasper groaned. "Dominique. Give me the phone right now." He didn't bother to keep the bark out of his tone.

She laughed this time, as if he'd just told the world's funniest joke, and held the phone out to him. He took it and glared at her before he left the table. The restaurant where they ate was certainly one of the five-star joints in Zurich, but he'd not enjoyed the food or the company.

"Sasha?" he said, relief in both syllables as he stepped outside.

"Who was that?" Her frosty tone carried all the way from Hawaii.

"You would not believe me if I told you." He sighed and ran his hands down his face, the fact that she'd called him comforting and...nice. It felt nice to have her reach out to him when he felt like he was the one constantly going after her.

"Tell me anyway," she said.

"There's nothing to tell."

"Jasper," she said, and while he may not have had a girlfriend in a while, he could definitely detect the fury in her voice. "My boyfriend's been gone for almost a week, and it's two days from Valentine's Day, and when I call, I get a giggly woman with an accent. You better start talking right now."

"Look who's being brazen now."

"Jasper."

"Are you jealous?" The night in the city was cold, but cheery with all the lights on the buildings shining into the darkness.

"You know my last boyfriend cheated on me, right?" Her voice was made of desperation, and he sobered.

"I'm not cheating on you," he said. "I would never do that."

"Keep talking."

So Jasper did, telling her all about his parents, their perfect little cottage snuggled into the snow, and the not-so-perfect woman his parents had decided was "the one" for him. "I'm on a flight in the morning," he said. "That'll be about nine o'clock tonight for you. And I'll be home late tomorrow night. I promise." Just in time for Valentine's Day, he wanted to add. But he didn't, because he'd been so busy here dealing with business and Dominique and everything else that he hadn't had any time to plan anything romantic back on the island for him and Sasha.

"You promise?" She sounded so small and so far away, and Jasper's heart squeezed. He wasn't entirely sure when she'd wormed her way inside his life, but he liked her there. Liked feeling like she needed him, as he hadn't felt needed by anyone in a long time.

"I promise," he said again. "Will you be free for dinner on Tuesday?"

"What's Tuesday?" she asked, followed immediately with, "Oh, yes. Valentine's Day. Yes. A late dinner, maybe?"

"Define late."

"I'm closing at eight. I'll be free after that."

"Sounds perfect." He gazed up into the sky, wondering if she could see the same stars as him. "I'll call you when I'm boarding, okay?"

"Okay."

They both sat on the line for a moment, and Jasper let the silence carry. It felt good to hear her voice, and he basked in the fact that he could just be himself with her, that he didn't have to talk to be comfortable.

"All right," he said as he turned back to the warmth of the restaurant. "I'll talk to you later." He ended the call and instead of going back in to finish dinner with Dominique, he turned away and started walking down the busy streets of Zurich.

The words he'd almost said bounced around inside his mind. "I'll talk to you later," he repeated. "Love you."

Did he love her?

He sure did like her. A whole lot. She *fit* with him, and he'd never had someone do that before. So while he'd considered leaving Hawaii only a few short weeks ago, he now knew he couldn't do it. Couldn't leave Sasha on the island and return to Europe, even if his schedule was weird, even if it would be easier to do business.

Because after a few days with Dominique, he knew he *really* liked Sasha, and he wanted to see if he could fall all the way in love with her.

———

Jasper woke sometime in the night, the country stillness of Bern surrounding him, suffocating him. His phone bleeped again, and he lifted it from the bedside table to find two texts from Sasha.

She tagged you in a photo, the first one read. *Looks cozy.*

The second said, *She might need to be told she isn't your girlfriend...unless of course, she is. Then just tell me I'm not, okay?*

Jasper didn't try to find the picture she'd referenced. He didn't care, because he didn't spend any time on social media despite having the accounts. He pushed his thumbs to type faster as he said, *You're my girlfriend. The end*, and sent it to her.

He really was too tired to deal with this, and he had to fly out in less than five hours. He exhaled as he laid back against the pillows again, knowing he wouldn't be able to fall back asleep, not after getting the flight in his mind.

If you say so, her next text read.

Jasper looked at the words and decided to randomly

change the subject. *I'm afraid to fly*, he typed out. The thought felt incomplete, but he sent it anyway.

You are?

"Deathly afraid," he whispered into the darkness as he put on the message. *So afraid I have to arrive really early just to get myself through all the security checkpoints on time.*

Only his mother knew this, and he wanted to share everything about himself with Sasha.

I've never told anyone but you.

Several long heartbeats passed, where he thought maybe he would be able to fall asleep again. Then his phone buzzed against his chest.

Thanks for telling me. Travel safe, and I'll be there to pick you up at the airport.

I have my car.

I'm picking you up.

A slow smile arched his lips. *Why? Miss me too much?*

Terribly.

The single word made his heart swell three sizes. *Don't you have to work?*

See you tomorrow, and Jasper chuckled at her finality. He also couldn't wait to see her, and he used her to get himself through the lines, checked in, and onto the plane.

He pressed his eyes closed and played his memories of her in slow motion as the plane took off, and before he knew it, the aircraft was landing, and he was getting off.

His body knew he'd been on a very long journey, but his brain didn't seem to care. All it wanted to do was find Sasha and kiss her.

When he heard his name, he spun toward the sound of

it and saw her. His beautiful, strawberry blonde girlfriend waved at him, and he broke into a run toward her. They laughed together as he swept her off her feet and hugged her.

"Hey," he said, setting her down. "Wow, it's good to see you." He hadn't realized how incomplete he felt in Switzerland, without her. He bent down and kissed her, right there in the crowded airport. She didn't seem to mind, holding the sides of his face as she kissed him right back.

"How was the flight?" she asked as she stepped back. Her dark honey eyes searched his face. "Not too terrible, I hope."

"They're all terrible." He grabbed the handle of his carryon. "I hate airplanes, airports, all of it." He headed for the exit, glad for the humid air as he stepped outside. The pent-up tension in his muscles started to seep away, and he sighed. "Solid ground. That's the way to go."

"Don't you fly a lot?" She dug her keys out of her purse.

"As little as possible," he said. "For a while there, I thought about moving back to Europe, to Belgium. But…." He trailed off, not quite sure how to articulate what he had here in Hawaii that he didn't have there.

"But what?" she asked. "Your sisters are over there."

"And I only get along with one of them" he said, seizing onto Danni as the reason he didn't want to move back. But she wasn't the reason, and Jasper knew it. Sasha didn't say anything else as they walked to her car.

"So." He blew out his breath and closed the trunk of

her car where he'd stowed his bag. "You're not working today. I'm exhausted and need to get my dog from Tyler's place. How about we then go to my place? Lay by the pool? Take a nap? Order food?"

She wrapped her arms around him and tipped her head back to smile at him. "That all sounds perfect." She separated herself from him and said, "You can tell me about your overseas girlfriend on the way to pick up Frankie."

Jasper choked, his mood darkening despite the idea of spending hours with Sasha, the sun, and his dog. "She is not my girlfriend, and there's nothing to tell." He marched around the car to the passenger side.

"You sure about that?" Sasha slid into the car and he followed suit. "She's posting about you all over social media. With heart emojis."

The headache Jasper had been fighting since the previous evening finally won, pounding through his temples and infecting his blood. "Sasha," he said in a weary voice. "Just because it's on the Internet doesn't mean it's true."

FIFTEEN

SASHA FELT about two inches tall. "No, I know," she said. Jasper closed his eyes and let his head fall back against the headrest. Foolishness snaked through her, but she couldn't stand to see that raven-haired beauty all cuddled up to her boyfriend.

He wore a happy smile on his face in all the pictures she'd seen, and he'd been dressed in his billionaire suits, his hair perfectly sculpted, and his eyes twinkling. Everything looked staged, right down to her diamond bracelet and the bright red lipstick she wore. So sickeningly, sweetly perfect.

Sasha's stomach coiled on itself. She didn't like the jealousy romping through her, or the way she couldn't seem to swallow properly. Jasper's breathing evened, and as she didn't know where Tyler lived, she headed toward Jasper's house in the hills. Once they arrived, she gently extracted his phone from his fingers and found Tyler's text string.

She let him know that he'd pick Frankie up in the morning if that was okay, and Tyler came back with *Sure thing, man. He loves it here.*

She felt like a snoop with his phone in her hand, so she set it in the cup holders between them and looked at Jasper. He wore no concern in his face while asleep, and she reached over and gently ran one fingertip along his eyebrow. He was so handsome, and so hardworking, and she could see why Dominique from Zurich wanted to post about him non-stop.

"Hey," she said gently. "Should we go in?"

Jasper stirred, but didn't wake. She couldn't very well leave him in the car to roast. Though it was only mid-February, the sun could still do some damage in Hawaii. So she leaned over and kissed him.

His lips stayed still for a moment, and then he woke. She pulled back, but he threaded his fingers through her hair and kept her close. "Mm." He moaned, and brought her mouth to his again.

"We're home," she whispered, realizing what she'd said a moment too late. Jasper didn't seem to catch the slip, because he just kept kissing her. Sasha let herself get swept away in the moment, because she didn't want to think about what it would be like to live here, in this huge house, with Jasper. As his wife.

Her heart beat faster and faster, though, reminding her that it was something they needed to think about sooner or later.

Later drifted through her mind. Right now she was kissing her boyfriend who'd been gone for a week.

She pressed her lips together after he finally pulled back. "Should we go inside?"

"Yeah." But he made no attempt to move. His eyes opened and he gazed at her, the moment soft and pliable. She liked it. Liked how comfortable she was, how they seemed to be the only two people on the planet, how he wore power suits and business smiles for everyone but her.

She straightened and opened her door, collected his bag from the back, and followed him up to the garage. He keyed in the code and the big door rumbled up. Four cars sat inside, in various sizes and colors. Sasha tried not to think about how just one of them would solve all of her financial problems.

"Do you have your suit?" he asked as he entered the mudroom off the kitchen.

"Nope." Sasha wheeled the bag inside. "It doesn't matter. I can just sun in my clothes."

His mouth opened like he might say something, but then he closed it again. She gave him a smile and said, "I know where the towels are."

"I'll get drinks." He stepped over to the fridge, and she wondered if he expected a fairy to provide something for him to drink. After all, he'd been out of town for a week.

She left him in the kitchen, the atmosphere between them suddenly more tense than she liked. Maybe because she was imagining him in his swimming suit—and perhaps he was doing the same thing.

She stepped onto the pool deck and took a deep breath. Several loungers bordered the pool and she chose one in full sun and draped a towel over it. Sitting on the edge of the pool, she put her legs in the cooler water, the peacefulness of this private oasis so relaxing. Her condo had a pool too, but there were always dozens of people there, many of them with little children.

Sasha's pulse pinched for a moment. Children. Did Jasper want kids? They hadn't spoken about it yet, and their relationship still felt pretty new to Sasha. He didn't come down for at least ten minutes, and when he finally joined her on the pool deck, he wore a pair of swim trunks the color of peaches and a dark gray rash guard that accentuated all the muscular ripples in his torso.

Sasha stared, unable to help herself.

"Sorry." He swept a kiss across her forehead as he sat next to her and took her hand in his. "I had to let my parents know I made it back safely. Well, my mom really. She's the only other one who knows how I feel about flying."

A frown sat between his eyes, even when Sasha reached over and touched him there. He met her eyes. "What's wrong?"

He shook his head. "I'm not quite sure."

"Something with your parents?"

"Maybe." He gazed across the pool and absently stroked his thumb over the back of her hand. "It's so good to be back here. It's cold in Switzerland right now. Snow and everything."

"Wow, snow." Sasha swung her legs in the water. "I think I've only seen snow in pictures."

"You're not missing much." He squeezed her hand and she laid her cheek against his bicep.

"Jasper?"

"Hm?"

Words crowded into Sasha's mouth, each of them jockeying for position to come out. She didn't want to tell him so explicitly how she was feeling about him, so she asked, "Do you see yourself as a dad?" instead.

"Yeah," he said immediately. "I mean...yeah. I'd like a kid or two." He bent his head to look down at her, but she kept her eyes on the fence in the distance.

"Me too," she said.

He put two fingers under her chin and lifted her face toward his. "So we're talking about serious things now." He wasn't asking, though his expression carried a question.

"Are we not being serious here?" Because Sasha felt two breaths away from falling in love with him, and she needed to do some serious backpedaling if he wasn't feeling the same things she was.

"I'm being serious here," he whispered.

"Good." She nodded and pressed a quick kiss to his lips. "Me too."

Several seconds passed before he said, "Wow, kids. Should we talk about where we might live when we get married?"

Sasha sucked in a breath, and Jasper chuckled. "Okay, I can see that's off the table for now."

"It's just—" She wasn't sure how to finish. He'd said *when we get married. When.* Not *if.*

"It's just what?" he asked.

"What makes you think you want to marry me?"

"I like spending time with you," he said, holding up one finger on his free hand. "I like kissing you." Another finger. "When I think of who I want to share my life with, it's you." A third finger. "We both like dogs, and want kids, and the beach, and I don't know. I think...maybe we won't get married right away or anything, but I can definitely see it happening."

He'd said so much, and Sasha took the time she needed to sort through it all. "Have you ever thought about getting married before?"

"To you?"

"To anyone."

"No." His voice was barely loud enough for her to hear. "No, Sasha. I've never met anyone I've thought about marrying...until now."

Until now.

The words seemed to echo in the sky above her, around her, inside her mind. *Until now. Until now.*

Sasha knew she wasn't quite ready to be married. The jealousy over Dominique's social media posts alone proved that. She also didn't want to bring any debt into the relationship, and right now, she couldn't do that. She didn't want Jasper's money to fix her problems.

But she kept those worries and admissions quiet and snuggled deeper into his side.

"What about you and Newt?" he asked. "Were you guys talking about getting married?"

"No," Sasha said. "Newt isn't the type to commit like

that. When he told me as much, I thought....” She let her mind flow back to that time to truly try to figure out how she'd felt. “I thought I was okay with it. Like, I didn't need a diamond to feel loved.”

“It's not the diamond that does that,” he said.

“I guess you would know,” she teased. “Being the diamond king and all that.”

He chuckled. “I'm not a diamond king.”

She straightened and looked at him. “I do want a diamond though. I mean, not right now or anything. But the more I think about it, and with what happened with Newt and all that, I know now that I do want to get married. Have a family. The fairy tale perfect ending. All of it.”

For the first time in her life, Sasha felt like she deserved all of it.

“And I'm sure you'll get it.” He pressed his mouth to her forehead and tucked her back into his side without promising anything else.

A few minutes later, they both moved to a lounger, where Jasper slathered sunscreen on the bare skin he showed and promptly fell asleep.

Sasha closed her eyes, wondering if this could be her reality one day. If this could be her pool. Her lazy afternoon alone with Jasper, her husband....

Her thoughts followed her into her dreams, and in those, the man, the money, the babies, the happiness hovered on the horizon, just out of her reach. No matter how she strained, stretched, or prayed, she couldn't touch them.

SIXTEEN

JASPER COULD ACCOMPLISH a lot in a short amount of time. Well, his money could. Even when the florist insisted she couldn't get an arrangement put together for Valentine's Day—which was the very next day —she suddenly could when he mentioned a price tag in the thousands.

He didn't care how much it cost to get him the table he wanted at Sasha's favorite restaurant, or if he had to fake sickness to get out of his business dealings. He wanted everything on February fourteenth to be absolutely perfect.

Jacqueline made heart-shaped pancakes, scrambled eggs, and orange juice and then conveniently disappeared with Jasper's envelope of money mere seconds before Sasha keyed in the code to the front door.

He hadn't put a list of chores on the table today, and instead, he leaned in the archway leading to the kitchen to watch Sasha put her bag down and gather her hair into a ponytail. She seemed tired, yet she was still so beautiful.

In those slow seconds while she searched the table, before she looked at him, he wondered if the pittering in his pulse and the softness in his expression was what love felt like.

"Hey," she said when she found him loitering in the doorway, still dressed from his conference calls the night before. "There's no list."

"Nope." He held out his hand, a clear indication for her to come with him. "I thought we'd have a romantic breakfast. Then you can shower and get over to The Straw. I'll sleep. And then I'll come hang out with you this afternoon before we go to dinner."

She inched toward him, her smile spreading across her whole face. "Oh, you've got plans, is that it?"

"Mm." He received her into his arms and kissed her. "Big plans." He laced his fingers through hers. "And they start with pancakes and juice. So come on."

The flower arrangement sat on the end of the counter too, and she gasped when she saw it. She went over to it and plucked the card from the blooms. The tropical arrangement was the most popular, according to Betty-the-floral-lady, and Jasper had gone with hit.

"I love orchids," Sasha said, selecting a bright pink one and leaning over to smell it. "These are for me, I assume."

He stood behind her, and wrapped his arms around her waist as she opened the card. "They're for you." He breathed in the soft, fresh scent of her skin, getting a hint of lemon and other citrus with it. They swayed together and the rush of affection cascading through Jasper's whole body could only be described as love.

Right?

He'd never felt like this about anyone before, but as she read his card, leaned her weight into his chest, and let him nuzzle her neck while she giggled, he was sure he was in love with Sasha Redding.

And if not, wow, love must be a powerful thing that few ever felt.

"Thank you." She turned and kissed him fully on the mouth, and Jasper enjoyed the moment, glad he had someone to share Valentine's Day with. He usually ignored the whole holiday and had Jacqueline make something for dinner the night before that would last so he didn't even have to leave the house.

"You wanna eat?" he asked after she'd kept her arms around his neck and leaned her forehead against his for several long seconds.

"Yes." Her voice sounded a bit rough around the edges, but he decided not to ask about it. She'd tell him what she wanted to tell him, when she wanted to say it.

She laughed when he pulled the heart-shaped pancakes out of the oven. "I'll be sure to tell Jacqueline thank you," she said with a flirtatious glint in her eye.

"How do you know I didn't make these?"

"Because you can't even make toast."

"Yes," he said. "Yes, that's one thing I *can* make." He chuckled. "And I happened to make the orange juice this morning too." He pulled the bottle out of the fridge.

"That doesn't need to be made," she pointed out.

"Fine. I bought it." He grinned at her and dished up some food for the both of them. "Tell me how you feel about gemstones." He didn't look at her though he could feel the weight of her gaze on him.

"Gemstones?"

"Yeah. Jewelry is a completely appropriate gift for Valentine's Day."

"Oh, the flowers—"

He pinned her with a look then. "Are you going to tell me I can't buy a gift for my girlfriend on Valentine's Day?"

A blush filled her cheeks. "No." She drew the word out. "But it's really not necessary. I'm not the kind of woman that needs a gift for everything."

"Noted." He slid the syrup toward her and joined her at the bar. "Do you like surprises?"

"Who doesn't like surprises?"

He laughed and cut the curve off the top of his first hearted pancake. "I'm sure there are people." He ate for a minute, and then asked, "Do you even wear jewelry?" He hadn't seen her wear rings or bracelets. Earrings, from time to time, when they went out. But at The Straw, she was bare from wrist to lobe.

"Not a lot," she said. "My hands get so dirty at work, and I'd hate to lose a valuable gemstone or something."

So a necklace would probably work. Jasper nodded and ended the questions in favor of feeding bits of egg to Frankie.

Later that day, while Sasha was at work and he'd slept as much as he was going to, he entered his jewelry shop on the island. He had very little to do with the day-to-day operations of the Rosequist retail arm of the company, but he did deal with the regional manager at the store. She took care of the hiring, the scheduling, the payroll, all of that.

And he did expect to be noticed and recognized in the shop he owned. It seemed busier today than any other time he'd come in, which was to be expected.

Three salespeople were helping customers, and there were two others browsing cases on their own.

GloraJean looked up from the case where she stood with a man and said, "I'll be right with you, sir. Oh. Jasper. Hello." She made to move toward him, but he held up his hand as if to say, *It's fine. Take care of him first*, and she nodded.

Her customer turned out to be painfully indecisive, because both of the other sales associates finished before her, assisted the other customers, and had just turned toward him before she'd even completed the sale.

"Jasper," the man said. His name tag read Malachi. "How are you?" He shook hands with Jasper and added, "What are you looking for?"

"A sapphire," Jasper said, deciding on the spot. The brilliant blue stone would look great on a silver chain, around Sasha's neck.... "On a necklace." He'd looked through the cases and only seen sapphires in ring settings. "What can we do to make that happen?"

Malachi smiled and gestured with his head toward the back of the store. "Well, you may or may not know that we just had a shipment of gemstones come in. Some of them might be intriguing as pendants."

Jasper's eyebrows went up. "Intriguing. I like the sound of that." He followed Malachi to the back of the shop, where he pulled out a case that had several loose pieces. GloraJean joined them and said, "It's good to see you, Jasper."

"Busy today."

"Valentine's Day." She peered at the case and the blue gem Malachi selected. "Are we doing a pendant?"

"Yes, ma'am." Malachi was polished from his crisp haircut to the perfectly straight tie around his throat. "This one would look nice on a slimmer chain. Let me show you."

Jasper let Malachi do his job, and sure enough, the sapphire was exactly what he wanted. While the piece was cleaned and boxed for him, Jasper wondered if he could be cheesy that night and tell her he hoped she'd wear it close to her heart and think of him whenever she did.

Was he that brazen? She claimed him to say whatever he wanted, but he wasn't sure he could say such things without uttering three more words that seemed little but that totally weren't.

Deciding to play it by ear, he took his gift and left the shop. His phone buzzed, and surprise bolted through him when he saw Brighton's name on the screen. It was barely four o'clock in Hawaii, which meant it was four a.m. in Paris.

Her text read *How was Mom when you saw her?*

Fine, he tapped out, frowning at his phone. *Obsessed with setting me up with a Swiss banker. But other than that, fine. Why?*

It took too long for Brighton to reply, but Jasper employed his patience. After all, it probably took a few seconds to send words so far.

Dad just called and said he's taking her to the hospital.

Jasper's heart stalled, first at the thought of something being wrong with his mother and secondly, it was way too soon for him to get back on another airplane.

I'm sure she's fine. A little flu or something. I'll keep you updated.

Day or night, Jasper said. Honestly, he didn't sleep much, even with the blackout curtains and the best ocean wave sound machine money could buy.

Brighton didn't respond, and Jasper wasn't sure what to do with the information. Call his parents? His father wouldn't answer if he was at the hospital. He'd probably left his device at home, though he claimed to take it with him everywhere. In the few days Jasper had visited them, he'd seen the phone lying on the end table more often than not. Once, he'd picked it up and it was dead.

So a call would be fruitless.

He made his way over to The Straw, where Sasha worked the window, wearing a cute purple visor and fabric hearts pinned to her apron as she passed two drinks to a man and his significant other.

Jasper hung back and watched her work, the look of happiness on her face clear even from a distance. She exuded charm for her customers, and she worked with quick, precise movements, her smile never far behind her words.

She worked through the line and leaned her hip into

the counter as a sigh escaped her lips. He couldn't hear it, but he'd seen that face before. The one rimmed with exhaustion and yet still so hopeful, so beautiful.

He pushed away from the tree where he'd been standing in the shade, and his movement caught her eye. A grin split her face and she turned to the woman she worked with and spoke to her. She untied her apron and then came through the door on the side of the stand.

"Hey." She practically skipped over to him, and he kept his hands in his pockets so he wouldn't grab onto her and swing her around.

"Hey, yourself. Happy Valentine's Day." He leaned over and kissed her, a quick peck.

"We've already had breakfast together. Or have you forgotten?"

He simply smiled and nodded down the beach. The sun went behind a cloud, and he wondered if it would rain. He actually hoped so—way down deep so Sasha wouldn't know—because then she might close her drink stand early and he'd get her undivided attention for a bit longer.

"Do you have a minute to walk?"

"Yeah, we're not too busy today," she said. "Maybe once school gets out, the teenagers will come over." She put her hand in his and they stepped through the sand.

"You seem quiet," she said after several paces. "Everything okay?"

"My sister called," he said as the sky darkened further. "My father's taken my mom to the hospital."

"Oh, no." She paused and squeezed his hand. "Is she okay? What happened?"

Jasper really liked her concern, and he once again had a flash of what his life might be like if Sasha was in it permanently.

"I'm not really sure. I'm waiting for more information." He took a deep breath and pushed it out. "When can you get off? I'm dying for our alone time." He swept his arm around her waist and brought her close to him.

She giggled. "I have to stay and see how things go with the after-school crowd. If things aren't too bad, I can take off once Macey comes."

"You sure? I don't want to rush you, and our dinner reservation isn't until eight-thirty."

"Where are we going?"

"It's a surprise. You said you liked surprises." He laughed at the put-out look on her face and tugged her further down the beach, something gnawing at his gut that he hoped would disappear before he sat down at Turf's Up, the best steak and seafood restaurant on the Big Island.

SEVENTEEN

SASHA GOT SLAMMED after school with teenage couples who seemed like they'd figured out more about love and romance at age sixteen than she had at age thirty-two. At their age, she'd painted The Straw a bright, cheery yellow and rented her first six blenders with her mother's credit card.

Nevertheless, she served everyone who came through the line with a smile, telling them about the bowling alley and movie theater at Sweet Breeze. Several of them took the coupon cards Fisher had given her, and she saw a decent number of her own half-price flyers come in as well.

Then the pre-dinner crowd arrived. And as reservations surely had to be staggered tonight, it seemed like the number of people lined up outside The Straw would never end.

Jasper had stopped texting about six, and a twinge of

guilt and worry needled her. She'd promised Macey she'd be off by eight, and with only fifteen minutes until closing, it seemed impossible that they'd be finished in time.

Especially when two more couples joined the line.

"Never gonna happen," Macey muttered as she stuck another ticket in front of Sasha. "Better cancel your big date."

"It's not a big date," Sasha said over her shoulder as the girl moved back to the counter. And she wasn't going to cancel it. She was going to work like mad and get through this rush and then close as fast as possible.

She had four blenders going, and she felt like she had the arms of an octopus as she made drinks and handed them out.

Miraculously, twenty-five minutes later, the line was gone. "Quick," she said before the last customer had even taken two steps. "Close the window. I'll clean up. You can go."

Macey had a boyfriend of her own, as evidenced by the twenty-something who emerged from the shadows and helped her lower the window opening and lock it into place.

Sasha took one moment to look around the interior of The Straw and decided to do only the bare essentials to get the place closed. She ran all the blender containers under water and put all the fruit in the fridge.

A quick wipe-down, and she hurried to untie her apron and hang it by the door. So she smelled like citrus and coconut milk. Jasper had once said that he liked the way she smelled, and she called him as she hurried across the sand toward her car.

"I'm done," she said. "Only fifteen minutes late. Where are you?"

"I'm at your place," he said.

"I'm five minutes away, and I just need to change."

"I've already called the restaurant."

Relief rushed through her. "I'm really sorry," she said.

"No need to apologize."

She couldn't tell if he was cool or simply unruffled. He had a way of coming off a little wooden, a result of his multi-million dollar diamond deals, no doubt. But she sometimes had a hard time deciphering his reaction when she was with him in person. On the phone, it was impossible.

She waved to him, sitting in his silver sports car, and ran inside to change. Five minutes—she gave herself major kudos for how fast she could brush her teeth and put on a dress, heels, and earrings—later, she hurried across the parking lot and slid into the passenger seat.

"I'm so sorry." She felt put together too quickly and sure had some piece that was out of place. Still, she flashed a smile, glad when he returned it.

"You're ready?" he asked.

"Yes." She noted that he didn't say her tardiness was fine this time. She straightened her skirt and leaned toward him, further relieved when Jasper closed the distance between them and kissed her.

"Mm," he said against her lips. "Worth the wait."

Warmth filled her from head to toe, and she straightened in her seat. Jasper extended a black velvet box toward her that was too big to hold a ring.

She gave him a coy smile as she took it. "I can't wait to see what this is." Her heart flopped around in her chest like it wasn't anchored properly. She took a quick breath through her nose to center herself, noting that Jasper hadn't started driving yet. So her lateness didn't seem to matter.

The lid creaked as she cracked it, and the brilliant blue stone winking back at her stole her breath. Before she could touch it, Jasper took the box gingerly, saying, "It's a sapphire. I thought a necklace might be something you could wear to work."

He lifted the silver chain from the silky folds of fabric inside the box, and she leaned forward, holding her hair back so he could put it on her. Their close proximity and the intimate nature of his fingertips along her neck made the moment heated and charged.

"I was thinking...." He ducked his head, and he was the most adorable man she'd ever met. Her heart throbbed in her chest, the sapphire hot against her skin.

He lifted his eyes back to hers. "I was thinking that you'd wear it close to your heart and think of me."

Sasha couldn't think of anything to say to such perfect words. So she pressed her lips to Jasper's, this Valentine's Day better than any other she'd ever had.

And the night only got better when he pulled up in front of Turf's Up and went inside with her hand securely held in his.

———

A few days later, Sasha was absently wiping down the counter while a slow drizzle fell beyond the window. It had been her slowest day since meeting with Fisher, and the rain wasn't helping matters.

Or maybe it was.

Because she couldn't stop thinking about Jaasper. About the careful, adoring way he'd kissed her on Valentine's Day. Or the passionate, heated way he held her when he'd kissed her good-night.

Her hand drifted to her mouth, and she yanked it back at the smell of wet rag mixed with pineapple. "Ugh." She put the washcloth in the sink and washed her hands, though she'd already done so about five times.

Part of her wanted to close up for the day, though it was only three p.m. She'd sent Maddy home, and Macey wasn't due to arrive for another two hours. But if she closed now, maybe she could sit beside Jasper's pool, despite the rain, and relax.

She felt like the only time she truly let her hair down and forgot about her worries was when she was with Jasper. She wondered what that meant, but the thoughts had swirled through her mind until late at night, and she needed all the sleep she could get.

Making a snap decision, she hurried outside and closed the window, making sure to lock it tight. She didn't need a CLOSED sign, but she did need to clean up a bit and send a few texts. Once that was done, she drove up into the hills to Jasper's house. She hadn't texted him, hoping he liked surprises as much as she did.

She fiddled with the sapphire against her collarbone as she sat in his driveway. Sometimes he texted her this early in the day, especially on Fridays, as he didn't work overnight from Friday to Saturday.

After letting her fingers drop from the necklace, she gathered her courage and got out of the car. She knew the code to the front door, but she knocked anyway. Nothing stirred behind the huge, heavy wooden doors. She tried the doorbell next, but was met with the same silence.

So she'd have to text him, ruining the surprise. Before she could, the garage door to her left started rumbling as it lifted.

She went back down the steps to find Jasper behind the wheel of a big, boxy SUV, his phone at his ear.

In the next moment, her phone rang, and she realized he was calling her. "Hey," she said, moving to catch his eye so he'd stop. "I'm on your front porch."

He whipped his attention back toward the house, braking hard enough to make a squealing sound. She lifted her hand and lowered her phone. He got out, and she took one look at him and knew something was wrong.

"Hey," she said casually anyway.

"Sasha." He engulfed her in a hug, and his pulse beat like hummingbird wings against her cheek. "I'm flying back to Switzerland," he whispered into her hair. "My mother is ill, and I need to go."

Sasha gripped him tighter, knowing how much he disliked flying. Her first inclination was to offer to come with him, but she had no money for the ticket and no one to run her stand while she was gone.

"I'm sorry."

"I was hoping to see you before my flight." He stepped back, seemingly undisturbed by the drizzling rain. "Why aren't you at work?"

"I decided to close for the day." She indicated the bad weather. "Come surprise you and see if you wanted to eat pizza beside your pool."

A fond smile adorned his face, but it wasn't strong enough to push out the anxiety. "That sounds nice. But my flight is in ninety minutes."

"You go," she said. "I know how to get into the house." She put on a smile, hoping it would be enough to take with him across the ocean.

He kissed her, this one with an edge she'd never felt before. Desperation, maybe. Worry. Fear.

She tried to soothe him without words, but he looked just as tense when he finally waved and got behind the wheel of his SUV again. She watched him go, her arms wrapped around herself and not only because of the chill in the air.

"Keep him safe," she whispered to the banyan trees in his front yard. She didn't really believe the plane would go down as it flew across the ocean, but Jasper did, and he was the one who mattered.

She turned back to the house, because his place was more comfortable than hers and she was already here. He didn't mind, and he did have that swimming pool....

———

Sasha couldn't remember the last time she'd taken a few hours and done nothing with them. Probably when Newt convinced her to let Amber run the stand alone while they hopped on a plane and went to the island of Lanai for the day.

The wind had been calm and the sun perfect. Sasha had thought there wasn't a more perfect man in the world, and she'd started dreaming in diamonds after that date.

Too bad she found out that Amber had stolen half of the day's profits while Sasha was out of the stand. And then that she'd slept with Newt while Sasha made sure everything was ready for the following day.

Or maybe it was good she'd found out before too many commitments had been made, more money lost, and last names changed.

No matter what, when she woke up from her poolside nap, Sasha felt relaxed and refreshed in a way she hadn't since discovering Newt and Amber's deception. She started flipping through her social media accounts, double-tapping to like Stacey's beautiful banquet spread for the beach wedding she'd had at Aloha Hideaway on Valentine's Day.

There were a lot of Valentine's Day pictures, and she wondered why she and Jasper hadn't even thought to take one. Sasha spent a few minutes on her social media each day, but she rarely posted anything of her own. She was of the opinion that only the good should be posted online, and she honestly hadn't had anything all that great in her life for almost a year.

But Jasper…he was the best thing that had happened to her, maybe ever.

She sighed and scrolled, almost putting her phone down to close her eyes again, bask in the affection she felt for the diamond-dealing billionaire who may have stolen her heart.

But a picture caught her eye. She knew that long, dark hair. The rugged, sexy square jaw of the Italian man she'd kissed so many times she lost count.

Newton's hair was slicked back, and pure joy radiated from his face as he looked at the camera. He wore a white shirt, black bow tie, and black suit jacket—clearly a tux. And Amber, the blonde he'd run off with, beamed out of Sasha's phone, her up-do, flawless makeup, and white dress all punching Sasha right in the chest.

Then the gut.

Then the lungs.

The caption was in Italian, which Newt had always promised to teach Sasha but never had, but she didn't need to be able to read it.

He and Amber had gotten married. Married, when he'd told Sasha for months that he wasn't the type to settle down, didn't want all the strings marriage licenses and I do's brought. Then it was that he didn't have the money to buy the diamond he wanted for her. The excuses were endless, and somehow, Sasha hadn't been able to see them for what they were at the time.

She could now, with a quick swipe to the right

revealing a rock the size of a bowling ball on Amber's manicured finger. Fine, it wasn't that big, but the diamond certainly wasn't small.

Sasha felt about two inches tall, and her breathing didn't seem to be bringing in enough oxygen.

Because she suddenly knew—Newt wasn't the marrying type, didn't want to settle down, or spend his money *on her*.

But for Amber, who he clearly loved, he did all of the above.

A sob tore through Sasha's throat, more angry than sad. "Why does he get to be happy?" she asked the pool water. The sun had started to peek through the clouds, and a bit of light made dazzling patterns over the bright blue water.

"Why does he just get to move on? Why does he still have power over me?" She wiped her face quickly. She would not cry over him. Oh, no, she would not. He would not beat her, though he'd taken her money and left her heart a shredded mess.

She tapped out a message to Jasper, knowing he wouldn't get it for hours, but hoping he'd respond as soon as he landed in Switzerland.

———

Several days later, Sasha lay in her beach chair, her legs extended in front of her, trying to soak up as much sun as possible. The other Women's Beach Club girls were all there, but the talking had died about a half an hour ago.

With three of them so blissfully happy, there wasn't much to detail these days.

In fact, Sasha had done most of the talking. She'd told them about Jasper's mother, and how they were still running tests to find out what was going on with her. How worried he was. How they talked every morning, and he texted her constantly.

Stacey had asked if Sasha would soon have an engagement ring, but Sasha had just shook her head no, Newt's traitorous face floating through her mind. She had not mentioned his recent nuptials to her friends, and the conversation had turned to Stacey's wedding preparations.

She'd booked her own gardens at Aloha Hideaway for the blessed event, and it was only creeping up on them now. They'd talked through it all—the dress, the bridesmaid's fittings, the hairstyles, the makeup artist, the flowers, the food. Honestly, Sasha thought Stacey's original idea to elope sounded a lot better than planning a wedding.

"His parents want to come," she'd said when Esther had asked about that. Stacey had been engaged twice before and had always vowed to simply elope if she found someone for a third time. But she'd been wearing Fisher DuPont's diamond for eight months now, and she'd become his wife in only one more.

Sasha was happy for her friend; she was. She was simply still grappling with the idea of love and if she even knew what it was, or how it felt. She'd thought so with Newt, but he'd duped her so completely, she wasn't sure anymore.

She knew when she pictured her life, Jasper was at her side. Her thoughts began to tumble in that direction when Tawny nudged her with her foot.

Sasha turned toward her and opened her eyes to find Tawny holding out her phone. "You're gonna want to see this."

Sasha took the phone as the other three women perked up. "What is it?"

"Tyler sent it to me."

Her phone had a picture on the screen, an obvious screen shot from the header and partially cut off caption at the bottom.

A picture of Jasper and Dominique. They were pressed cheek-to-cheek, smiling like their lives depended on it, and he looked anything but "exhausted" and "worried" as his last text to her that morning had said.

Numbness spread through her though it was one of the warmest days they'd had in a while. She was so tired of being flayed open by social media.

But she couldn't help reading the caption she could see. "Celebrating Valentine's Day a little late with my *Schätzchenli*! So glad he's back from...."

She handed the phone back, wondering what *Schätzchenli* meant. Probably boyfriend.

What if it means fiancé?

Sasha's heart turned to ice, and she got up. "I'll be right back." She gripped her phone like she was trying to choke the life out of it.

"Sash," Tawny called after her, and Sasha heard the other girls ask to see the phone as she walked away.

She didn't care what they thought. But she would not be cheated on again, not here beneath her nose and not halfway across the world.

So she dialed Jasper's number, not caring at all that it was two-thirty in the morning and she might wake him.

EIGHTEEN

"DAD, YOU SHOULD REALLY CONSIDER MOVING." Jasper mixed too much sugar into his coffee and watched his father. He'd been having the same conversation since he'd arrived in Bern six days ago. His father's face fell, the first indication Jasper had that he might actually be thinking about it.

"It's just like Bern," he said. "A quiet atmosphere. Quaint houses, right on the beach, if that's what you want. There's no snow."

His mother had fallen on a patch of ice in the driveway, prompting their initial trip to the hospital. But they'd kept her due to some abnormal blood work. Since then, they seemed to take more blood than she had to give, running test after test.

They were supposed to get the final results that afternoon.

"I'm there," Jasper said. "And I'm not going to leave."

The thought had been circling his mind since he'd gotten on the plane in Hawaii. Life would be much easier if he lived in Europe, from the work hours to being able to help his parents.

But Sasha was not in Europe, and Jasper always came back to her when the idea to leave Hawaii started growing.

"Mom would love it," Jasper continued as if his father had engaged in the conversation. When he stayed silent, Jasper decided to let the subject sit. His phone went off, but as he kept it on silent in the house, only the screen flashed.

It wasn't Sasha, and he didn't really care to talk to anyone else. Especially Dominique, who'd sniffed him out almost the moment he'd landed. He wasn't sure why she was so interested in him—he'd told her multiple times he had a girlfriend in Hawaii—but she didn't seem deterred.

She was smart, and beautiful, and someone out there would be lucky to have her. But for him, there was simply no spark there. He doubted he'd be able to feel anything for another woman again, as he'd given his heart to Sasha.

He finished his coffee and they went to the hospital. His mom seemed in good spirits for the most part. She'd been up and had started walking around, but she still wasn't...right. Jasper wasn't sure what was wrong, only that he knew something was.

She wasn't herself, and it wasn't only because of the bruised hip. They visited all afternoon, and still the doctor didn't come in. He entertained himself by texting Sasha, who would be up in an hour or so. She'd said she liked waking up to his name on her phone, and he'd been sure to text her between five and six every evening so she'd have messages to read when she got up.

Tonight, he told her he was tired, exhausted really, and worried about his mom. He glanced up at her and found her studying him with a curious look on her face.

"Mom?" Maybe she'd said something to him and he'd been so absorbed in his phone, he hadn't heard her. She'd been napping for a couple of hours but was wide awake now.

"Harold?"

Jasper flicked his eyes to his father, whose sandy hair like Jasper's had gone white decades ago.

"Mom, I'm Jasper." He took a step toward her like she was a tiny rodent he didn't want to scare away. But alarms sounded all through his body. This was so much more than a physical ailment. This was dementia. Alzheimer's. Something. Panic followed the alarms, and Jasper worked to keep his voice even.

"Do you know who I am?"

She blinked and it was like the light bulb had been turned back on in her brain. "Of course I know who you are. A mother knows her only son." She looked at her husband, who frowned but said nothing.

He nodded to the hall and said, "Dad and I are going to go get the nurse and see if she kept your dinner." He barely waited for the door to close before rounding on his dad. "Did you hear that? She thought I was you."

"She's just confused."

Jasper settled his weight on one foot. "Dad."

"She's fine, Jasper." But he wrung his hands like he knew there was something wrong too.

"Dad." Jasper put one hand on his father's shoulder, once so powerful, so authoritative. He spoke kindly when he said, "I don't think she's fine, Dad. How long has she been confusing things?"

"I don't know. A few months. When you were here before, she kept saying that she hoped you'd bring Dominique to Danni's wedding."

Jasper pulled in a breath. "Danni's been married for nine years, Dad."

"I know. She was just confused." His father looked at him with those same dark green eyes Jasper had, begging him to say everything would be okay. But Jasper had a feeling everything was about to change.

He turned away from his father, unable to give the comfort he wanted, and said, "I'm going to go find out why the doctor didn't come this afternoon." He half-expected his dad to come with him, not trusting Jasper to talk to the right person or get the job done correctly. But he just drifted back into the hospital room where his wife lay, and Jasper realized how old they'd gotten.

His heart squeezed and pinched. Oh, how he loved them and wanted to be there to take care of them. "They have to come to Hawaii," he muttered to himself as he walked over to the nurse's station.

"Excuse me," he said in German. "We're still waiting for an update on my mother, Joan Rosequist?"

The nurse gave him a friendly smile and searched through the charts on the desk in front of her. "Doctor

Osbourne got called into emergency surgery," she said in accented English. "Let me see if there's someone else who can go over the test results with you."

Jasper nodded, not sure what else to do besides lunge for the file, grab it, and start running.

Another hour passed before someone poked their head into the room. "Joan Rosequist?" The man wore a long, white coat like doctors in the movies.

Jasper stood quickly and said, "Yes," energy suddenly rushing through his veins. "I'm her son, Jasper Rosequist." He indicated his father. "Her husband, Harold."

"I'm Doctor Tony." He shook all of their hands, the folder tucked under his arm making Jasper jumpy. He finally stood beside Jasper's mom and looked down at her. "I'm afraid I have some bad news. It's good you have your family here with you." He looked at Jasper and then his father.

"I'm sorry to say that the blood work we've done has not shown us anything. Your PET and MRI scans are inconclusive. But as a leading neurologist, it's my belief that you have Parkinson's Disease."

A low wail started in Jasper's ears. "But you don't know for sure," he said, his voice belonging to someone or something outside his body.

"Parkinson's is very difficult to diagnose," Doctor Tony agreed. "So I'd like to put you on a drug specifically for Parkinson's and see if there's improvement. Often, when there is significant improvement on the medication, that can be basis for a sure diagnosis."

His mother looked up at Jasper, tears glinting in her

eyes and the most childlike expression on her face he'd ever seen. "What's he saying, Jaspy?" She hadn't called him by his boyhood nickname since he was twelve and insisted she stop since the older boys at school had started teasing him about it.

"He's saying he's going to give you some medicine so you'll get better, Mom." He reached for her hand and squeezed it tight. "Okay?" He nodded at the doctor. "Let's try the medication."

By the time he returned to the cottage and got his father properly tea'd up and in bed, Jasper's exhaustion had reached an all-time high. Or low. Or whatever. He could barely think, but there was so much to do.

He'd been working shortened hours during the day, drinking coffee just after noon, and heading to the hospital for afternoons and evenings.

Desperation surged up his throat and hot tears pricked his eyes. While he was going to wait to see if the Parkinson's medication helped, he felt certain his mother had the debilitating neurological disease.

He hadn't had the heart to bring up moving to Hawaii after he and his father had left the hospital. His dad had looked so...broken, and Jasper had never seen him like that.

"I'll ask him in the morning," he told himself as he changed into gym shorts and a T-shirt. He really wanted to talk to Sasha, but it was almost noon in Hawaii, and she'd surely be busy with the lunch crowd who wanted drinks to take to the beach.

Dominique's name and picture came up on the screen,

and Jasper tossed the phone to the bedside table in the guest bedroom where he'd been staying. The woman had impeccable timing, and he couldn't deal with her right now. Couldn't deal with anything right now.

Just focus on what's in front of you, he thought, something his parents had taught him growing up and into adulthood as his dad trained him in the dealings of the diamond mines.

And right now, what was in front of him was a good night's sleep. He wouldn't be much good to anyone if he was a zombie, so he got in bed and forced himself to sleep.

———

His phone rang sometime later. Odd, was his first thought, as he kept the phone on silent in the house. But it certainly wasn't quiet now as another peal rent the air.

He sat up and scrambled to find the device on the bedside table. The deep darkness surrounding him should've told him it was an emergency and he should answer it straightaway, but he still checked the screen to see who was calling.

"Sasha," he breathed out as he answered the call. "Hey."

"Hey?" The anger in the word soared across the space between them. "Hey, yourself, *Schätzchenli*."

Confusion swept through Jasper. He pulled the phone away from his ear and looked at it. It said Sasha's name, but he'd never heard her speak like that. When he put the device back to his ear, she was already talking.

"...go back over there just to be with her? You should've just told me. I don't need your pity, and I certainly don't want to be lied to."

"What?" he asked, unsure of what in the world she was talking about.

"Is she there right now? Is that why you're not saying anything?" She gave a mirthless laugh. "It's two-thirty in the morning, Jasper."

"Is who here?"

"Dom-i-nique." She clipped out each syllable separately.

"Sasha, I have no idea what you're talking about."

"I'm sure that's convenient for you."

Jasper exhaled and hung his head, still utterly confused but too tired to have this conversation. When he'd seen her name, he'd thought she'd be the one person in the world to give him the comfort and support he so desperately needed.

"I'll text you." She hung up before he could even think of a response. He stared at the now-black device, his eyes adjusting back to the darkness everywhere. It took a few minutes for his phone to brighten again, and when it did, the message was two words and a picture that started to download.

The words: *We're through.*

His heart ricocheted around inside his chest. "We're through?" he echoed, wondering how this day could get any worse.

Oh, but it could, because when the picture came up, his own blood boiled at the shot of him and Dominique on her social media feed. At first he was sure it was an old post, but then, when would he have spent any time with her at all?

He'd only met her the last time he'd come to Switzerland—and she was wearing that ridiculous pink dress she'd worn to their first meeting.

He practically punched the call button next to Sasha's name at the top of the screen. The call rang and rang, but she didn't pick up.

"Look," he said, his voice almost a bark. "That picture is from the first time I came to Switzerland. I've only seen Dominique once in the last six days, and we had glass between us while I passed her a folder at the bank. I swear. Please call me back."

He hadn't screwed this up. That picture wasn't his fault. And while he wasn't Dominique's *Schätzchenli*—treasure—he'd hoped he was Sasha's.

"Wishful thinking," he said, collapsing back onto the bed. Just like thinking he could get his parents to move to Hawaii, or run a huge diamond conglomerate from a tropical island in the middle of the night.

As Jasper lay there in the dark, he tried to feel something. But he was simply too stunned—and Sasha did not call him back.

NINETEEN

SASHA LISTENED to Jasper's message every day for a week, her fingers itching to dial him back. Talk to him. Apologize until he got on a jumbo jet just for her and came home.

But her pride would not let her, and she had to admit to herself why.

She wasn't ready to trust a man yet. Newt had carved open her chest and shattered something inside her that wasn't all the way healed yet, and she would not go back to Jasper until she was sure she could give all of herself to him, including her heart.

"Doesn't mean you can't talk to him while you heal," Esther said one afternoon as the two women sat with Stacey, sampling cakes for her upcoming wedding.

"I don't know," Sasha said. "What if I just drive him farther away?" Her jealousy had already reared its ugly head once before this. She'd overreacted then too, and she didn't trust herself not to ruin things completely.

"Maybe he'll understand." Esther put a big bite of the chocolate cake in her mouth. "Stacey, this one is divine. If you don't choose it, I'm having it at my wedding."

"When are you getting married?" Stacey lifted her eyebrows.

"Oh, I don't know." Esther lifted one bare shoulder and scooped up another bite of cake. "I haven't talked to Marshall about a date yet."

"I thought you wanted a summer wedding." Stacey tried a bite of the lemon cake, and she moaned. "This one is so great." She pushed the plate toward Esther and Sasha.

Honestly, all the cakes tasted the same to Sasha. Her taste buds—the one thing she'd been able to depend on through everything—had abandoned her. She put a bite of some pink cake in her mouth anyway and pretended to like it.

"I do want a summer wedding, but it's March already, and there's no time to plan a wedding by summer."

The door behind them opened and Tawny bustled through it, still wearing her cut and tied T-shirt with a pair of gray leggings. She rolled her eyes. "These two guys stopped me after class and asked *all kinds* of questions." She dropped her purse on the floor and took the seat next to Stacey.

"I think they're the developers of that new place over in the east bay."

Sasha perked up then. "There's a new place over in the east bay?"

Tawny picked up a fork and took a bite of the chocolate cake. "It hasn't been announced yet, but Fisher's had people over at his hotel. You know, men with fancy suits and one scary-looking woman in six-inch heels every time I see her, even in the sand." She shook her head. "I honestly don't get heels."

"Try the lemon," Stacey said. "You just need more cake and then everything will be okay."

Tawny took a bite of all the flavors, visibly calming with each one. She finally exhaled and said, "Okay, I feel better. So. What did I miss?"

"Esther thinks she can't plan a wedding by oh, September, which is technically still summer." Stacey rolled her eyes and stabbed her fork in Sasha's direction. "And Sasha's still not talking to Jasper, even though she's totally in love with him."

"Stacey," Esther said at the same time Tawny squeaked. Sasha felt like she'd been electrocuted, twice.

"I'm not in love with him."

"Are too." Stacey folded her arms and looked straight at Sasha. "Trust me, we've all been where you are."

Sasha's bottom lip started to tremble and she pulled in a deep breath to contain her emotions. "How do I get out of this place?"

Esther patted her hand and then squeezed it. "You'll figure it out."

Sasha wasn't so sure. In fact, all she was sure of was that she couldn't keep living like this.

———

Jasper called every evening for sixteen straight days. When he missed on the seventeenth evening, Sasha felt the loss of it keenly. A voice screamed in her head that she could call him. She knew how to dial a phone. But at this point, she didn't know what to say.

Jasper, on the other hand, true to his say-everything-he-thinks personality, left sixteen messages. Sasha didn't delete a single one of them, and while he seemed to be telling her about his mom and the plans they had to all move to Hawaii in a couple of months.

He talked about his work one night, and then his sister in Paris the next. He probably used a timer, because he spoke for about sixty seconds and then stopped just before the voicemail cut him off.

He talked about the picture and how it wasn't a Valentine's Day celebration and that he hadn't seen Dominique once since being back in Europe.

And the funny thing was, Sasha believed him. She just wasn't sure how to get out of her own way.

And Jasper stopped calling anyway. Two days went by. Then three. Then a week. She stayed busy as the weather warmed and as Stacey's wedding neared. Before she knew it, the day had come, and she sat in the chair with Tawny on her left and Esther on her right to get their hair done.

She felt like a third wheel, like she didn't belong in her own circle of friends anymore. Her left hand felt too light and she wanted to hide it in her pocket whenever the other ladies were around.

But the bridesmaid's dresses had no pockets, and she couldn't do anything about her naked ring finger. But as her hair got curled and swept up onto the top of her head, as the makeup artist somehow brought out the contours of her face that Sasha didn't even know she possessed, the magic of the day started to seep into her bloodstream.

She enjoyed herself as the ceremony got closer and closer. After all, she had great friends doing great things, and she was glad to be a part of their lives.

The wedding party walked down the aisle, and Sasha held her flowers lightly while she stepped beside Owen Church, Fisher's general manager from the hotel. She was supposed to be on Jasper's arm, and she felt the loss of him beside her keenly.

Owen looked every bit the same as the other billionaires in Fisher's party, and Sasha kept her smile pinned in place as she separated from Owen and joined the other girls. The wedding march began, and Stacey appeared at the end of the aisle that had been set up in the gardens.

The shade from the palms and banyans, along with the rows and rows of flowers, made the entire scene like a fairytale. Sasha watched her friend take step by careful step, beaming out at all the attendees, her arm looped through her father's.

They paused at the front of the group, where her dad leaned over and whispered something to her before kissing her cheek. Stacey grinned even wider then, and the smile almost split her face as her dad passed her to Fisher.

He also pressed a kiss to Stacey's temple and brought her directly beside him before they both focused on the pastor who stood behind a flower-laced altar.

He said a few words and then said, "It's my understanding that the bride and groom have written vows they'd like to read." He indicated they should do so, and Stacey took a slip of paper from her mother and faced Fisher, holding the paper with one hand and the microphone with the other.

"Fisher, when we first met, I was determined not to like you." Twitters sounded in the audience, but Stacey continued undaunted. "But because of your charm and caring way with everyone around you, somehow you wormed your way into my heart. I once followed you to Michigan to get you back into my life, and I'd follow you anywhere."

She paused, the emotion in her voice thick, but her words landing like bombs in Sasha's ears. Stacey had gone to Michigan to make things right with Fisher after a misunderstanding.

Jasper hadn't called or texted in a while, and Sasha couldn't expect him to jump on the first jet and come back to see her. She had no idea what he'd been dealing with in Switzerland after the diagnosis of his mother, and with his terrible fear of flying, he wouldn't come back to Hawaii until he was certain he wouldn't have to leave again.

If he came back at all.

He'd never given any indication in his texts and voice-mails that he wouldn't be returning to the island.

Stacey said something else about her love and devotion to Fisher, and he started to read his vows. But Sasha could only hear *I once followed you to Michigan to get you back into my life....*

Sasha needed to get to the airport as quickly as possible. Jasper couldn't come back though he probably wanted to. So she'd go to him.

But she couldn't run out on one of her best friend's weddings, either, so she kept her feet rooted to the ground, smiling and counting down the minutes until she could leave, pack a quick bag, pull out the credit card she'd stuffed in her nightstand drawer, and find the first flight to Switzerland.

TWENTY

JASPER PACED in the tiny guest bedroom, the date eluding him at the moment. It had been too long since he'd seen his beloved tropical island view from his back deck. The wind here was only cold. It didn't whisper through the trees and rustle the grasses that grew on the hill behind his house. It didn't push waves into neat patterns, or cause him to take a deep breath of the fresh air and be grateful for his island life.

At least his parents had agreed to move to Hawaii with him. He had a massively huge house, and they could live on the main level easily, where he could watch over the pair of them. His father had spent so many years of his life as the stoic, know-it-all, businessman that Jasper didn't know what to make of the frail, older gentleman who couldn't seem to make a decision to save his life—or his wife's.

So Jasper had been doing all of that. All the paperwork.

All the questioning. All the phone calls, the texts, the emails, the arrangements with the realtor, everything.

The house had sold in only a week, even with the winter. He'd been packing and cleaning for weeks, and Brighton had flown in to help as well. But she brought her kids, and it seemed like they were taking one last vacation to Switzerland instead of helping.

They'd come over in the evening, bearing dinner, and then she'd talk to their parents while Jasper took care of more business. After all, moving everything his parents owned over the course of their lifetime was no easy task.

"Eight more days," he muttered to himself, the stillness of the countryside here a tad bit unsettling. Eight more days, and he'd be back on the airplane he hated, but at least he'd be going home.

With the thought of home came Sasha, and he wondered if he'd be daring enough—brazen enough—to stop by The Straw for something to drink. Maybe take his parents so they could try the Cancer Killer, meet his girlfriend....

"She's not your girlfriend anymore." And that thought sent him spiraling, wondering if he could just get on a plane, go see her, make her understand, and then come back to finish everything up. If only he wasn't so terrified of plummeting into the ocean from forty-thousand feet in the air.

He couldn't stand the thought of flying on top of everything else, so he pulled back on all the thinking and opened the door.

He'd taken two steps before Brighton appeared at the end of the hall. "There you are. Dad wants to see us all."

"All right." Jasper tugged on the bottom on the T-shirt he'd just changed into. He hadn't brought enough clothes to spend six weeks in Switzerland, and he'd bought several things here. The T-shirts didn't fit him in the arms and chest correctly, but he had nothing else to wear, so he entered the kitchen feeling a bit out of sorts.

"Danni's on the phone." Brighton held it up, and she said, "Jasper's here now, Danni."

"Hey, Jasper."

"Danni." Jasper loved his sister, but he didn't enjoy spending much time with her. She and her husband lived in Belgium. They'd come to visit twice since the diagnosis, but she ran a high-end fashion school, and she couldn't be gone for long.

"We're all here, Dad." Brighton looked at her father, who lifted a teacup to his lips and took a shaky sip.

"I just want all of you to know that we've redone our will."

Jasper's heart pumped out an extra thump. "Dad."

"We're not signing over the power of attorney until we get to Hawaii," he said. "And that's still the plan. We appreciate all you've done for us, Jasper."

Brighton met his eyes, and he was glad she wore a glint of anxiety as well. "What are the changes?" she asked.

"Nothing too major," his father said. "Jasper is still the sole heir of the family business. But we have certain assets we'd like to be divided up between the three of you."

"Dad." Jasper pulled out a chair and sat down at the

table with the other members of his family. "You're not dying any time soon." He threw a quick look at his mother, who sat very still at the table, her eyes alert. She was having a good day so far.

"We just want everything in place, and we want everyone to know about it." He surveyed the group again. "Do you want to tell them, dear?"

Jasper's mom smiled at her husband. "My family came from wealth, too," she started, and Jasper leaned forward, having never heard this story before. Their money came from the diamonds, which had been in their family for generations.

"Mom." Brighton covered her mother's hand, her voice hushed.

"We've been investing the money for quite some time, and we want to split it three ways and distribute it as soon as the power of attorney forms are signed." She glanced at Jasper and then Brighton. "It's a considerable amount for each of you."

"Mom, we don't need the money."

"Invest it for your families," their dad said. "That's what we've done, and it's made quite a bit of profit."

A stab of longing hit Jasper right behind the lungs. He had no family to pass his fortune to, and he wondered how he could go back to Hawaii and carry on as normal without Sasha in his life.

It seemed every conversation somehow led him back to Sasha.

"How much money, Mom?" Danni asked through the line.

Jasper almost rolled his eyes. Her fashion firm did just fine, but of course it would be her asking for the amount.

"Five hundred million each," his mom said, and Jasper almost fell out of his chair.

"Dad." He stared at him. "Is that true?"

"Your mother has an excellent mind." He reached over and covered his wife's hands with both of his. "She handled all the investments for sixty years. This is her life gift to you."

Brighton sniffled, and Jasper himself was having a hard time keeping his emotions contained. She hugged their mom, and Jasper didn't know what to do.

Five hundred million dollars. Money couldn't buy love, but it could pay off debts and alleviate financial burdens. Sasha swam in his mind's eye as he blinked back tears.

He had to do something to get her back into his life, and while he couldn't stomach the thought of getting on an airplane, he could try calling her again.

The conversation seemed finished, so he stood and said, "I need to make a call," and stepped out onto the front porch. The evening air felt like ice in his chest, but he didn't return for a jacket. He dialed Sasha, almost desperate for her to answer though it was early in the morning in Hawaii.

But the line just rang and rang, leaving him frustrated and wondering what it would take to get her to pick up the blasted phone.

He managed to school his voice into a sort of calm submission before he said, "Hey, Sasha. It's Jasper. Not sure if you still have my number in your phone." He cleared his throat, the idea that she'd erased him from her life so, so painful.

"Anyway, I'm coming back to Hawaii in eight days, and I'm bringing my parents with me. I'd love to have the house prepared for them." He pressed his eyes closed with the ease with which he'd resorted to treating her like his employee.

Of course, she was his housekeeper, and if he hadn't gone and fallen in love with her, he would've asked her to prepare the house.

But he had fallen in love with her, and she was so much more than his housekeeper.

"I mean—" He had no idea what he meant, or what to say. He just wanted her back. So he said, "I just want to see you. Talk to you. Be with you." His voice failed him after that, so he hung up and squeezed the phone until he felt the plastic give just the teensiest bit.

———

Sasha didn't call him back in the middle of the night, or the next morning. He honestly hadn't expected her to, but the insane part of him that still dared to hope was doing exactly that. It hurt when his hopes were completely dashed, but he went through the tasks for the day with his heart beating in his chest somewhat robotically.

Near dinnertime, about the time he expected Brighton to show up on the doorstep with takeout, the doorbell rang. He didn't even look up from the folder he was reading. This, at least, wasn't something about his mother's health, with big medical jargon he didn't know off the top of his head.

Still, the report out of the Antwerp diamond operation required his full attention. The doorbell rang again, and he called, "Just come in, Brighton." She'd have her kids with her, and surely they hadn't gotten so much food that one of them couldn't open the door.

"It's not Brighton."

Jasper looked up at the female voice, his heart zinging around in his chest. It couldn't be....

He leapt from the barstool and strode through the living room, wondering where his parents had gone. He remembered his father had said something about a museum as he reached for the doorknob, not daring to hope that Sasha stood on the other side.

It's not her, he told himself. And if it was Dominique, he'd slam the door in her face. He'd met with her once after Sasha had broken up with him, and presented her with legal papers to take the pictures of him off her social media accounts. They'd all been deleted within the hour.

The doorbell rang again, jolting Jasper out of his mind. He twisted and pulled, not breathing as the door opened to reveal who stood on the front steps.

"Sasha." Her name fell from his lips the way a star falls from heaven, and he wasted no time gathering her into his arms and taking a deep breath of her skin, her hair, her. "You're here." He held her away from him, her ponytail swinging with the sudden movement. "What are you doing here? Why didn't you call? I'd have come met you at the airport."

She gazed up at him, her dark honey eyes twinkling yet filled with trepidation at the same time. "Oh, you hate airports, and I figured out how to drive on the wrong side of the road well enough. Well, there was that one car that seemed quite angry at me...."

He couldn't take his eyes off of her. "I hate airports." Pieces clicked around inside his head, but they didn't come together to make a complete picture.

"Right." She looked past him. "Is it possible to go inside? I don't know how to survive in the cold."

"Oh. Right." Jasper jumped back, pulling her with him into the house like she might make a mad dash for it if he let go of her. "What are you doing here?"

"I came to see you," she said, tucking a stray piece of hair behind her ear. She wore a black coat that didn't seem like it fit well, a pair of jeans, and black boots. Lines of exhaustion sat around her eyes, and he wanted to bring her close to his chest and protect her from everything bad in the world.

He simply kept his hand in hers and watched her. "I called you a kajillion times."

"First, a kajillion doesn't even exist." She removed her hand from his and unbuttoned the coat. "And second, I would've answered the last one, but I was on the plane."

"Did you get my messages?"

"All of them." She met his eyes, something fearful swimming in hers. "I'm sorry," she said. "I know you didn't have anything going on with Dominique. I just...I don't quite know how to trust men like you."

"Men like me?" Jasper folded his arms. "What kind of man am I?"

"A rich man."

Jasper opened his mouth to say something, but nothing came to mind.

"I just…. So I was at Stacey's wedding, and she read her vows to Fisher, and she said something about how she'd gone to Michigan to get him back into her life, and as I stood there in these *awful* heels." She rolled her eyes as if heels were the worst imaginable footwear on the planet. "All I could think about was coming here to get you back into my life. I'm not perfect." She swallowed and wrung her hands together. "Not even close. I know that. I'm in debt up to my eyeballs, and I don't love you for your money. I need time to learn to trust, but you said once that you weren't going anywhere."

Jasper heard so many things, he didn't know which one to focus on.

All I could think about was coming here to get you back into my life.

She wanted him in her life?

I don't love you for your money.

She loved him?

"So." She took a big breath and clenched her arms across her chest. "Are you staying here or are you really coming back to Hawaii with your parents?"

He swept his hand toward a pile of boxes in the living room, the only answer he could give in his current condition.

She *loved* him?

Her eyes traveled over to the boxes, and he found his voice. "The movers are coming in a week. We fly out the next day." Just saying the word *fly* made his stomach clench.

Sasha nodded and returned her attention to him. "So, this looks like a pretty small cottage. How do you feel about an additional houseguest for the next week?"

Jasper could answer that non-verbally too, so he cupped her face in his hands, his brain finally aligning all the thoughts, all the words, and turning them into action. "Oh, there's no room here. But I'll get you a hotel in town, okay?"

She put her arms around his neck, her eyes drifting closed as she nodded.

"And Sasha?"

"Hm?"

"I love you too." He kissed her then, the taste of her, the smell of her, the way she felt against his chest, absolute perfection and everything he'd been hoping for.

TWENTY-ONE

"IT IS NOT HAPPENING, so put it out of your mind."
Sasha glared at Jasper, the man she'd just flown hours and
hours to see and pushed her food around her plate. His
sister had shown up only a few minutes after they'd made
up, and while Sasha had wanted to kiss him for a lot
longer and then have him take her on a tour of Bern, that
hadn't happened.

Introductions were made, and then his parents got
home, and dinner was served. They all crammed into the
tiny kitchen, where Jasper had thrown a wrench in the
conversation by saying, "Oh, and I just came into a bunch
of money and I'd like to invest in The Straw."

Like it was nothing.

Like Sasha and The Straw had dozens of billionaire
investors banging down the door.

But she wasn't going to take a single dime from him. At

least not right now. She must've glared hard enough, because he dropped the subject.

"Should we go see about a hotel?" he asked several minutes later.

She nodded, gave his sister a hug, and left with him. "How do you want to drive?" she asked.

"Depends."

"On what?"

"On how long you'll let me stay." He gave her a wicked grin and pulled her close, his hand along her waist so welcome. It had been too long since she'd seen him and she made a mental vow never to let herself get into that dark place where she'd been for the past six weeks.

"You can stay as long as you want," she said. "I mean, not overnight or anything. I don't want your mom to think I'm that kind of girl." She gave him a flirty smile. They'd never talked about sex, but Sasha had barely started along the track to fully trusting Jasper. So she knew she wasn't ready for much more than kissing, and talking, and then more kissing.

And that was exactly what they spent the rest of the evening doing. By the time Jasper said, "I'll just take the rental back to my parents' place and come get you for breakfast," Sasha felt sure she'd entered an alternate reality.

After all, she'd never used her passport before. Never flown across the ocean. And never told a billionaire that she loved him.

Maybe she was the brazen one after all.

Seven days in Switzerland turned out to be too short to see everything she wanted to see, do everything she wanted to do, kiss Jasper at all the beautiful places she wanted to kiss him.

Before she knew it, she stood in the security line with him, his parents in front of them, while Jasper tried to squeeze the life out of her hand. She didn't tell him it was okay. She simply talked to him like normal, asked him his plans for the rest of the week, and if he really wanted her to come clean for him.

"No," he said. "You don't need to do that anymore. Wait." He peered at her. "You still can. I know you need the money."

She did need the money, but she said, "I think you'll need a few days to get settled with your parents. Then we can talk about it."

They'd talked about a lot of things in the past week. He'd brought up everything—her family, his family, children, her job, his job, their odd hours, all of it.

Well, not all of it. The topic of diamonds and weddings had *not* been discussed, and Sasha really wanted to get it out in the open. She waited until they'd boarded the plane and put on their seat belts before she turned to Jasper and said, "So, are you going to take me to your jewelry shop and buy me a diamond ring when we get back to the island?"

He blinked at her for a couple of long seconds before a

laugh spilled from his mouth. "Oh, you want to get married, do you?"

"We've talked about it before," she said as the rumble of the engine built beneath her. The plane moved, and Jasper didn't seem to notice.

"I'm just wondering if you've ever thought about your wedding," she said.

"Not particularly."

"Well, it's April already, and I've sort of always wanted to have a holiday wedding. You know, Christmastime?"

He did that blinking again. "You're thinking eight months from now?"

"Too soon?"

"I haven't even asked you yet."

She giggled and laid her head against his shoulder. "Well, you better get on that then. I've seen you pull together last-minute plans like a champ. I'm sure you'll think of something before we land."

His eyebrows shot sky high. "You want to get engaged when we get back to Hawaii?"

"Of course not." She lifted the armrest as the plane turned and then paused. In the next breath, it accelerated, pushing her back against the seat, where she snuggled into Jasper.

His chuckle turned into a gasping inhalation, and he tightened his arm around her shoulders. "I hate taking off."

"But I distracted you all the way until then." She tilted her head back and he touched his lips to hers.

"I guess you are good to have around," he teased just before he kissed her again.

————

Jasper did not ask Sasha to marry him when they landed. Instead, she watched him fly into oldest son mode as he took care of his parents' every need. They were hungry? He got them whatever they wanted to eat. His mom was too hot? He turned on a fan. They wanted the royal tour of this house? He led them around with the exuberance of a child on Christmas morning.

Sasha enjoyed watching him with them, actually, and she was quite happy to trail along. She saw the pure exhaustion come over all of them, and she felt it herself, so she gave him one final kiss and headed back to her condo.

She'd gotten Lexie of all people to run her stand while she'd been gone to Switzerland, and she found a folder containing all the daily reports for the past eight days, right down to the penny.

Sasha had asked the woman point-blank if she had a crush on Jasper, and Lexie had laughed in her face.

"We tried a relationship," she said when she'd finally stopped laughing. "There was nothing there for either of us. We're just in this club—" She'd clammed up at that point, and Sasha hadn't pushed the issue. But knowing Jasper had some secret club and he hadn't told her about it had caused Sasha a moment's pause.

But really, did she have to know everything about him?

In the end, she'd decided she didn't, and she'd gotten on the plane like she'd planned.

And she'd find out about the club, eventually. After all, she had a club of her own too.

She jolted away from the folder and opened her Women's Beach Club group text to let all her friends know she was back on the island, and yes, Jasper had come home with her.

Smiley faces and exclamations came through on the text, even from Winnie. Sasha practically floated toward her bedroom, where she collapsed and slept for a good long while.

TWENTY-TWO

IT TOOK a week for Jasper to re-acclimate to island life and get his parents all settled. They seemed to be enjoying the pool, as well as the trails around town up to waterfalls, the pineapple plantation, and the lava state park.

His mother had healed from her fall pretty well, and she still had a large percentage of good days. His father seemed to have snapped out of his funk, and he got his wife to doctor's appointments and made sure she took her medication.

Jasper got back to work, and he left a list for Sasha each day but he found himself too tired to see her before she went back to The Straw. When he wasn't sleeping or working or dealing with his parents, his mind revolved around how to ask Sasha to be his wife.

My wife.

Sometimes he paused in the middle of a task as the two words struck him with wonder. He somehow managed to keep up with work, but nothing had come for a grand proposal.

"Sasha doesn't need grand," he muttered to himself as he got off the elevator on the twenty-eighth floor at Sweet Breeze.

Laughter came through the ajar door, and he nudged it open and went inside. He hadn't seen any of his friends in the Hawaii Nine-0 club in weeks and weeks, and the sense of family and camaraderie that hit him square in the chest made him stall in the doorway.

"Hey, Jasper's back." Tyler approached, looking every bit the beach bum he tried so hard to be. But he walked with the gait of a man who'd worn expensive suits and ate at high-end restaurants quite a lot in his life.

The two men shook hands, and Jasper couldn't help grinning at Tyler. "So you're all made up with Tawny, I've heard."

"And you came back with your parents and your girl-friend." Tyler grinned and drank from his water bottle.

"Yeah." Jasper exhaled as Marshall and Lawrence walked over, still engaged in a conversation about the value of bitcoins in actual business.

"Hey, Jasper. Welcome back." They all shook hands, and Marshall added, "Fish said to say hello. I guess he's somewhere in France. Newly married, you know."

"I know." A twinge of guilt pulled through him. "I feel bad I missed the ceremony."

"Owen took your spot with Sasha," Marshall said. "It worked out."

"When are you getting married?"

"Oh, you know." Marshall looked over Jasper's shoulder as the elevator dinged again. "Whenever Esther tells me."

"She hasn't set a date?" Tyler asked.

"Do you have a date?" Marshall challenged as Lexie joined them.

"A date for what?" she asked.

"His wedding." Marshall cocked an eyebrow at Tyler.

"As a matter of fact, Tawny is thinking Christmas."

Christmas ran through Jasper's mind for a moment, and then Lexie said, "I thought you'd come home engaged, Jasper."

"Oh?" He studied her, not quite sure why she thought so or how she was privy to any information about his private life.

"Yeah, I worked The Straw for Sasha. Didn't she tell you?"

His mouth dropped open. "You ran The Straw?"

Lexie smiled and accepted the bottle of water from Agnes as she came over. "Yep. I ran The Straw, and Sasha told me everything." Her eyes practically danced with delight. She laughed and she and Agnes walked away, already engaged in some other conversation.

An idea struck him. "Lexie," he called. She turned back, her eyebrows raised. "I need some ideas for a proposal...."

He ignored Tyler's laughter and Marshall's "You take her to the jeweler and have her pick something out," and stepped around them to talk to Lexie.

———

Another week passed before Jasper's plans came together. Sure, he owned the jewelry shop, but he couldn't just happen to take her by and point to the cases like *Pick one out. I love you.*

It had to be more than that. Bigger. Better. Something that showed her he truly loved her, and would do anything to be with her.

Lexie proved to be helpful once again. She owned and operated one of the world's largest mutual fund companies, and she had some ways of finding information out, especially about Sasha's business. The two women had formed some sort of bond Jasper hadn't anticipated when he'd first asked Lexie to take a shift at The Straw so he could go out with Sasha.

She'd somehow managed to find out where Sasha's debts were and for how much. Jasper had bided his time as he made the rest of the plans, and finally, yesterday, he'd called and paid off everything.

When Sasha found out, she'd likely be furious, so he wanted to have the diamond on her finger before he told her.

To do that, he needed someone in the stand for her, where, once again, Lexie stepped in. To Jasper's knowledge, she hadn't dated anyone in a while, and he wondered if he was causing her any distress by asking for so much of her help. He didn't dare ask, though, and she didn't say anything.

He turned from the cases of diamonds in the shop and straightened his tie. His mother had chosen the bright orange paisleys on a shopping trip with Sasha, and it

STRAW AND DIAMONDS   227

paired nicely with his navy blue suit. He just wished his nerves hadn't come on so strongly.

But Sasha was late.

Of course, she didn't know it, but Jasper did, and he kept telling himself to hold on a little longer. If he could just make it through a few more minutes, he'd have himself a fiancée.

He took a long, deep breath and moved up one case to examine its contents. This one held red and white balloons, all the gems removed for the time being. The case in front of that, closest to the door, held a single envelope.

The chime on the door sounded, and Jasper glanced up to find Sasha standing there in a pair of jean shorts and a blouse the color of tangerines. She wore her hair up, like she'd come from work, which of course, she had.

She carried her purse slung over her arm, and she cocked her eyebrow at him. "What's going on here?"

"There's something for you in that case there." He nodded to the first one.

She moved forward, a bit of a smile on her beautiful face, and looked down into the glass. "I don't know how to open it."

"Oh, let me, madam."

She quirked a coy smile at him. "Madam?"

"I've worked a lot of hours in a jewelry shop. The women are always madam or ma'am." He slid open the glass in the back and picked up the envelope as if it were made of glass. "Try this one."

She laughed and took the envelope from him, her eyes barely leaving his as she flipped it over and opened it.

"Find the next envelope among the red and white." She nodded toward the next case. "I assume it's in there?"

Jasper swept his arm toward it in a grand invitation for her to help herself. "Right this way, ma'am."

She shook her head at him, though she clearly enjoyed this game. Jasper wasn't sure it wasn't the stupidest way on the planet to ask her to marry him, but he couldn't think of anything else and he didn't want May to come without making Sasha his fiancée.

After opening this case herself, she started removing the balloons from the case, the rubber edges of them squeaking as she squished them out of the small opening. It took her several minutes, but she finally found the envelope way over in the corner.

She made an exaggerated gesture of wiping her forehead like she'd just done something really hard, a giggle accompanying the opening of the envelope.

"Jasper." Her voice carried awe, and she stared at the paper in her hand while he dropped to both knees. "These are—" Her eyes met his, and she seemed to have been struck speechless.

"Sasha," he said. "I'm in love with you. I know you want to travel the world, and I want to be by your side as you do it."

She shook the stapled packet of pages at him. "There are a dozen airplane tickets here." A tear ran down her face. "You hate to fly."

He lifted one shoulder into a shrug. "But I love you."

She swiped at her face and sniffed. "I don't deserve this."

"Of course you do." He stood and swept her into his arms. "I love you," he whispered into her hair. "And you'd make me the happiest man on Earth if you said yes to being my wife."

She gazed up at him, love and adoration in her expression. "All right."

"All right?" he teased, bending down to kiss her cheek. "Like, all right, if I have to."

"No." She giggled and pushed against his chest. "I love you, too, Jasper, and I can't wait to be your wife."

A grin split his face, and he laced his fingers through hers and tugged her toward the third case. "So pick one."

She gazed into the case for a few minutes, moving left and right as she looked at the different rings. "There's another envelope in here." Sasha looked at him, and panic blipped through his bloodstream.

"That's for after you pick the ring," he said evenly as he moved behind the case as if he were the salesman. "Which one would you like to try?"

She pointed to one and said, "The one with the big one in the middle with the clusters on the side."

Jasper pulled the ring out for her and handed it to her to slide onto her own finger. Once she selected the one she wanted, he'd put it on for her, and kiss her, and then show her the last envelope.

Sasha went through several rings before declaring one that had come out of a mine in Australia "the one" and Jasper took it from her and polished it up nice. Then he slid it on her finger with the words, "So are you still thinking of getting married at Christmastime?"

"Yes," she said. "Too soon?"

"Sweetheart, I'd marry you tomorrow." He beamed down at her and then kissed his fiancée.

She seemed to melt into him, and he liked the way she poured everything she had into the kiss. When he pulled away, she whispered, "I want to see what's in that last envelope."

He chuckled, but it sounded a bit nervous to his own ears. But he retrieved the envelope and kept a tight hold on it before relinquished it to her. "I don't want you to be mad."

Surprise ran across her face. "Why would I be mad?"

He handed her the envelope and fell back a couple of steps. The sound of ripping paper met his ears, but he kept his eyes on her sandaled feet.

"Jasper," she said, a dose of exasperation in her tone. Then more flipping pages. "Jasper, these are my bills."

"Not anymore." He finally lifted his eyes to focus on her. "Because I paid them all."

Anger flashed in her eyes, but it went out quickly. "I didn't want you to do that."

"We don't always get what we want." He shrugged as if to say *What are you going to do about it?*

She took a step closer to him, and he had the distinct impression to fall back. But he held his ground as she stalked all the way too him and slapped his chest with this new sheaf of papers. Somehow, he'd made her cry again.

"I love you," he said for a third time. "And I have more money than anyone should ever have. Let me help you with this. Just this once." If she could tell he was lying, she didn't call him on it.

"You're almost too good to be true," she said, leaning into him in a coy, playful way.

"Oh, that's completely false," he said. "I work all night. I'm terrified of flying. I'm stubborn and do things even when you tell me not to. And let's not forget how I say whatever I want."

She laughed and tipped up onto her toes and kissed him. A slow, passionate kiss that erased all his concerns over her reaction to the paid bills.

"I love my brazen billionaire," she whispered against his lips before claiming them again. Happiness poured through him as he kissed his fiancée, sure they'd have a long and happy life together.

———

Read on for a sneak peek of Book 5 in the Getaway Bay Resort Romance series, **THE BILLIONAIRE CLUB**, where you'll get to meet a female billionaire and the man she almost married…

SNEAK PEEK! THE BILLIONAIRE CLUB CHAPTER ONE

LEXIE KELLER SAT at the vanity, applying her makeup in quick swooshes of the brush to properly contour her face. Some women were blessed with high cheekbones and a porcelain complexion, but Lexie took classes and spent enormous amounts of money to achieve those things.

Or at least the appearance of them.

As her fortieth birthday approached, she couldn't help feeling a little melancholy. She pushed the feelings away and swiped on a generous amount of the sparkly, razzle-dazzle lip gloss Sasha had given her for Christmas a few months ago.

Sasha Redding had come into Lexie's life quite unexpectedly, and through Jasper Rosequist of all people.

Still, her part-time job at The Straw now provided Lexie with the one bright ray of hope in her life—and how pathetic was that? And she thought she'd been boring as a penny pusher, a number lover, and a mutual fund heiress.

But the moment she stepped into The Straw, she felt lighter than she ever had. "Hey, girl," she said to Sasha, who was bent over a notebook at the back counter.

"Lex, how are you?"

"Doing great." Lexie had become an expert fibber over the years.

Why did you come to the island? Work.

Are you seeing anyone, dear? Yeah, Mom, I see men all the time.

No one had to know that yes, Lexie worked here on the island, but she could work from anywhere. And her mom didn't need to know that the men she saw were fellow Nine-0 club members who had zero romantic interest in her. And she wasn't interested in any of them.

"Brewing up something new?" she asked Sasha. The owner of the drink stand, Sasha had an incredible palate and an adventurous imagination when it came to fruits and flavorings.

"Maybe," she said, pressing the eraser end of her pencil against her temple. "I can't quite make it come together. But I think something new for spring would be nice. Get our customers back in here after this dreary winter.

The rainy season had been bad this year, and Lexie immediately thought about the people who'd been stranded up in the mountains after the landslides just after the new year. Thankfully, everyone had made it home safely, and Lexie had just read about one couple who'd met on the excursion, fell in love while they were stuck in a remote shack, and were now engaged.

So it proved that people could meet under the most

extraordinary of circumstances, and Lexie hadn't felt so foolish for thinking her one and only was going to come through the line at The Straw one day.

She tied an apron around her waist and faced the front of the building where the order window was. No one waited for a drink, and she asked. "How long has it been dead?"

"Only about ten minutes." Sasha seemed really distracted. "You'll be okay if I run out for a few minutes? I need to go pick up the Sunrise Special cards and take them over to Sweet Breeze."

Lexie opened her mouth to offer to take them later that evening, when she'd be in the owner's penthouse for her Nine-0 meeting. But the group was exclusive, and secret, and Lexie snapped her lips closed again.

"I'll be fine," she said instead and scraped her thick, dark hair into a ponytail on the very tippy top of her head. Sasha left without saying anything, her focus still on the notebook as she made her way up to the sidewalk and her car.

A couple appeared then, and Lexie put on her business face, one that wore a smile and did mental math and enjoyed being around other human beings.

For a while there, when she'd first come to the island, Lexie was sure she could be happy living in her spacious rambler, anonymously, on the south side of the island.

"Lemon Whip," she repeated. "And Berry Blast. That's eleven ninety-two." The couple paid, and she blended, and a line formed. Lexie kept her focus on what was immediately in front of her, but that didn't mean the dark-haired man loitering along the beachwalk, by the biggest palm, didn't catch her attention.

Of course he did, as it wasn't the first time Lexie had seen him in that exact position, leaning against the tree with one powerful shoulder, both hands in the pockets of his designer shorts, one foot crossed over the other at the ankle.

Jason Burnes.

If he thought for one moment she didn't see him when he spied on her, he was wrong. Her mouth filled with a sour taste that had nothing to do with the limes she'd just zested.

Jason had come to the island over a year ago, when Tyler Rigby—a fellow billionaire in Hawaii—had made up a fake engagement. Tyler and everyone else on the island knew Jason as a reporter for a poker magazine.

But Lexie knew him as a bartender in New York City, where she'd lived before making her big move across the ocean and leaving her high-rise life behind.

And the dangerous, abusive ex-fiancé that had ruined her so completely she hadn't been able to stay in a city of millions with him still there.

When Lexie finished with the customers, she stood very still in the window, shooting her best laser gaze toward where Jason stood against the tree. Almost a challenge. Like, *Well? What are you doing here again?*

He ducked behind the trunk, and a measure of satisfaction pulled through her. She'd never confronted him so fully before, and though thirty yards separated them, she felt a bit breathless and weak.

Why was he watching her? And why couldn't she have just let it go, like she had all the other times?

Sasha returned, asking, "How'd it go?" and Lexie snatched up the washcloth and started wiping the counter. She knew one of Sasha's pet peeves was a sticky, drippy service counter.

"Great." She wiped in circles, her eyes drifting back to that palm tree as worry gnawed at her insides.

———

That evening, Lexie straightened her blouse and patted her hair as Sterling, the valet at Sweet Breeze, got behind the wheel of her car. She loved coming to the Nine-0 meetings, and she'd held them at her house a time or two. They'd gotten a couple of new additions over the past six months, and Lexie had enjoyed making friends with the new women on the island.

But she wasn't as business-minded as most in the club, though none of them knew it. Sure, she knew what went on at Keller Investments, the huge financial resources company where she owned fifty-one-percent of the shares. But her oldest brother, Luke was the one who really ran things from their thirty-five-story building in New York, and her youngest brother, Bruce, was the CFO.

So her CEO was really in title only. Still, she had the right number of zeroes in her bank account, and no one really seemed to care what she did if she had that.

The lobby at Sweet Breeze seemed unusually quiet,

though she supposed for a Wednesday at almost nine PM, there wouldn't be much going on at the luxury resort.

She stepped past the public elevators and down a hall that led to Fisher's private one and pushed the button. The light flashed red, and she keyed in the code.

"Four-seven-six-two," a man said, and Lexie practically leapt away from him. She hadn't heard him coming, and her heartbeat rippled like a flag in a stiff breeze as she took in his tall frame, wide shoulders, dark hair, and the soapy, spicy scent of his cologne.

Jason Burnes.

"Are you following me?" she demanded, wishing the car wasn't already up on the blasted twenty-eighth floor. She really had to get away from this man.

"Not at all."

She cocked her hip, wishing his voice didn't reach right down into her stomach and make it vibrate in a good way. "Right. I saw you at the beach today." *And every other day I work,* she thought but kept to herself.

"It's a public beach." His dark eyes that had once consumed her so completely while she sipped seltzer water flashed, and she recognized the danger in them. She didn't trust journalists, especially ones who came to the trade after five other attempts at a career in wildly different fields. So her money could buy her some information, something she didn't go around flaunting but which she also didn't ignore.

"What do you want?" she asked.

"Do you know who I am?"

"Of course I do."

Surprise lifted his eyebrows, and a softness she hadn't expected entered his eyes. "How's Luke?"

"Better now that you're gone." The elevator chimed and the doors started to slide open. She stepped inside, intending to leave without another word. The likes of Jason Burnes didn't deserve a good-bye or a nice to see you. Because she wasn't glad to see him.

And he'd gotten bolder, approaching her in this tiny hallway. Or maybe it only felt tiny because he was so big, so broad, and still so beautiful.

She shook her head as she punched at the only button in the elevator, the one that would take her to Fisher's penthouse.

"I didn't leak that story," he said. "I quit instead of talking to the police."

Their eyes locked, and Lexie wanted to believe him so, so badly. Her heart thundered like water roaring over cliffs.

"Lex." The agony in his voice wasn't hard to hear, but Lexie only lifted her chin, determined not to show him that she still had feelings for him.

The car doors slid shut, removing the handsome face of the only man Lexie Keller had ever truly loved from her sight. The elevator moved, and Lexie slumped against the back wall.

It was ridiculous how easily he could remove her every defense. How her hopes skyrocketed just from the nearness of him. That her feelings, though seven years old, were still there, just dormant.

The elevator beeped again, opening to reveal the door

to Fisher's penthouse. Lexie smoothed her hair again and faced her future: making drinks to stay social during the day and attending secret meetings with her friends at night.

There was absolutely no room for Jason. Not again.

———

"You wanna come?" Gabi, one of the newer members of the Nine-0 club, pulled her shirtsleeves down and looked at Lexie. "You can just have coffee."

Lexie smiled and nodded as she shouldered her purse. Gabriella Rossi was an old friend whose family had made their fortune in cruise ships. So she knew Lexie didn't drink much more than champagne, and even then she usually just held the glass so people wouldn't pester her about drinking more.

Her father had been an alcoholic, and a mean one. So while Lexie loved her parents, she didn't love what alcohol had done to her childhood.

"Are you okay?" Gabi put her hand on Lexie's elbow. "You've been distracted all night."

"It's...." Lexie met Gabi's lighter brown eyes, hers more the color of caramel while Lexie's were like black coffee. When Gabi had first come to Hawaii, Lexie had panicked. She didn't want anyone living on the island who'd known her in her previous life. But everything had been fine, and Lexie had worried needlessly.

Maybe Jason would be like that.

No. She shook her head. "Another old friend has come to the island."

Gabi linked her hand through Lexie's arm. "Intriguing. Male or female?"

"Male."

Gabi nodded to Ira, who set his glass on the credenza and joined them as they walked out. She and Ira had started seeing each other about six weeks ago, and the atmosphere felt a bit awkward as the three of them loaded onto the elevator.

"Do I know him?" Gabi asked, always the lover of games, especially riddles and puzzles.

"I don't believe you do." Lexie had kept her relationship with Jason under wraps as much as possible. As her younger brother's best friend and a man way below her father's standards, Jason had agreed to keep their dates, hand-holding, and kissing behind closed doors.

She went to his place, or the bar, or they met somewhere at odd hours. He never came to her place, or picked her up, or pressed her against her front door and kissed her goodnight.

"You don't sound happy about him being here." Gabi stepped out of the elevator with Lexie, leaving Ira to follow along like a puppy.

"I'm not."

"Was he more than a friend?"

Yes. "No."

"Well, that doesn't give me much to go on. I assume you haven't mentioned him to me."

"No." They reached the front doors and Lexie paused,

the scent of Jason's cologne hanging in the air. It took all of her self-control not to start swiveling her head back and forth to find him. "I'm not feeling up to coffee. I think I'm coming down with something. You two go on."

Plus, she didn't need to be the third wheel with Gabi and Ira when their relationship was so new. Perhaps she could call Sasha and see if they could grab a late night snack together.

But she and Jasper were together now, and Lexie stood in the brightly lit foyer, wishing she had someone to go home to as well. Drawing in a deep breath, she stepped out to the valet, expecting to see Sterling but coming face-to-face with Jason instead.

"What are you doing here?" she demanded even as she scanned him from head to toe and found him wearing the service clothes of someone who worked at Sweet Breeze.

"I work here," he said needlessly, his eyes devouring her too. She wished she didn't like it so much, crave his attention so strongly, or know exactly where to find him next time she wanted to see him.

He grinned at her as if he could see all of her thoughts inside her mind. "Do you need your car?"

————

Read THE BILLIONAIRE CLUB today to see if Jason and Lexie get their happily ever after!

BOOKS IN THE GETAWAY BAY RESORT ROMANCE SERIES

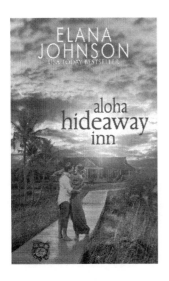

Aloha Hideaway Inn (Book 1): Can Stacey and the Aloha Hideaway Inn survive strange summer weather, the arrival of the new resort, *and* the start of a special relationship?

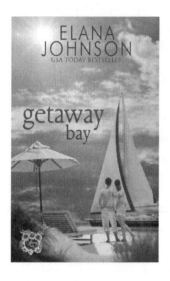

Getaway Bay (Book 2): Can Esther deal with dozens of business tasks, unhappy tourists, *and* the twists and turns in her new relationship?

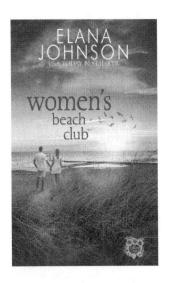

Women's Beach Club (Book 3):
With the help of her friends in the Beach Club, can Tawny solve the mystery, stay safe, and keep her man?

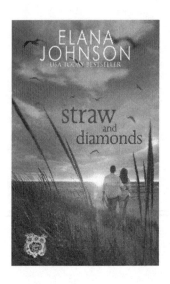

Straw and Diamonds (Book 4): Can Sasha maintain her sanity amidst their busy schedules, her issues with men like Jasper, and her desires to take her business to the next level?

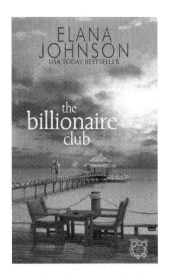

The Billionaire Club (Book 5): Can Lexie keep her business affairs in the shadows while she brings her relationship out of them? Or will she have to confess everything to her new friends...and Jason?

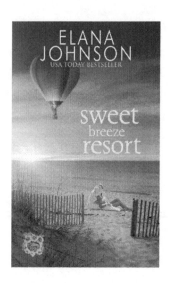

Sweet Breeze Resort (Book 6): Can Gina manage her business across the sea and finish the remodel at Sweet Breeze, all while developing a meaningful relationship with Owen and his sons?

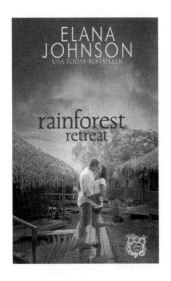

Rainforest Retreat (Book 7): As their paths continue to cross and Lawrence and Maizee spend more and more time together, will he find in her a retreat from all the family pressure? Can Maizee manage her relationship with her boss, or will she once again put her heart—and her job—on the line?

Getaway Bay Singles (Book 8): Can Katie bring him into her life, her daughter's life, and manage her business while he manages the app? Or will everything fall apart for a second time?

Turn the page to view series starters from three of my other series!

BOOKS IN THE GETAWAY BAY ROMANCE SERIES

Escape to Getaway Bay and meet your new best friends as these women navigate their careers, their love lives, and their own dreams and desires. Each heartwarming love story shows the power of women in their own lives and the lives of their friends.

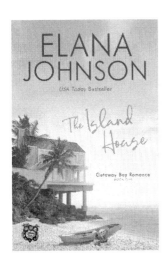

The Island House (Book 1): Charlotte Madsen's whole world came crashing down six months ago with the words, "I met someone else."

Can Charlotte navigate the healing process to find love again?

BOOKS IN THE STRANDED IN GETAWAY BAY ROMANCE SERIES

Meet the McLaughlin Sisters in Getaway Bay as they encounter disaster after disaster...including the men they get stranded with. From ex-boyfriends to cowboys to football stars, these sisters can bring any man to his knees when the cards are stacked against them.

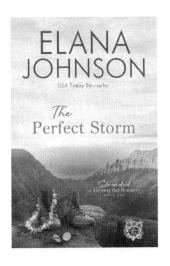

The Perfect Storm (Book 1): A freak storm has her sliding down the mountain...right into the arms of her ex. As Eden and Holden spend time out in the wilds of Hawaii trying to survive, their old flame is rekindled. But with secrets and old feelings in the way, will Holden be able to take all the broken pieces of his life and put them back together in a way that makes sense? Or will he lose his heart and the reputation of his company because of a single landslide?

BOOKS IN THE HOPE ETERNAL RANCH ROMANCE SERIES

Love cowboys and the beach? The Hope Eternal Ranch series combines them both! You'll get a sweet and sexy hero in every book as, one by one, the Mulbury boys get released from the low-securty prison in the Coastal Bend of Texas and go to Hope Eternal Ranch, where they find their second chance at life, love, and happiness.

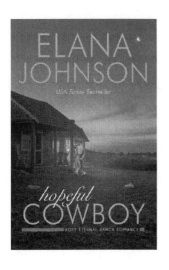

Hopeful Cowboy, Book 1: Can Ginger and Nate find their happily-ever-after, keep up their duties on the ranch, and build a family? Or will the risk be too great for them both?

ABOUT ELANA

Elana Johnson is the USA Today bestselling and Kindle
All-Star author of dozens of clean and wholesome
contemporary romance novels. She lives in Utah, where
she mothers two fur babies, works with her husband full-
time, and eats a lot of veggies while writing. Find her on
her website at feelgoodfictionbooks.com

Made in the USA
Las Vegas, NV
07 October 2023